Sgt. Janus

RETURNS

SGT. JANUS RETURNS
©2020 Jim Beard

A Flinch Books Production
Flinch Books and the Flinch Books logo
© Jim Beard and John C. Bruening
www.facebook.com/flinchbooks

Expanded Edition

Previous edition published by Airship 27 Productions in 2014

Cover illustration and design by Jeffrey Ray Hayes
PlasmaFire Graphics, LLC
www.plasmafiregraphics.com

Interior layout and formatting by Maggie Ryel

ISBN: 978-0-9977903-5-1

*For the Little Woman, who always seemed to know
what it was like to live in Edwardian times...*
Jim Beard

TABLE OF CONTENTS

Letters to the Editor

Dear Sir,

After much careful thought I feel very strongly that I must add my voice to the growing number that is currently calling for the wrecking ball to visit the property at No. 4 Raynham Road. While the ill-pedigreed structure was occupied, it was an eyesore and a blight on the countryside, but now as it is allegedly abandoned by its owner, it should be quickly razed so as not to become a haven for hooligans and opiate-users. As a community, we should act and act swiftly on this matter.

My family has lived for multiple generations on the land adjacent to that of the so-called "Janus House," and we have more recently suffered for that unfortunate proximity. Roman Janus was a man of questionable background and even more mysterious and dubious profession, and his habit of bringing all manner of "clients" to his residence brought to my mind many questions of impropriety and even possible illegalities. Why, once we even witnessed gypsies camping out on his front lawn! Add to that the unexplained noises at all hours of the day and night and the rumors of a woman living in the house with Janus – unchaperoned! – and you have a picture of a situation that could not stand. And, now, I say that the house itself should not stand if its master no longer cares enough for it to occupy it and maintain it. Though, of course, I say he did not maintain it even when he sat in residence there.

Is it not the responsibility of the people of the good town of Mount Airy, a respectable and proper community, to take this matter in hand? I sit on several committees and plan to bring the question up as many times as is necessary so that people will come to realize that we have an opportunity to correct a great injustice to our fair town – and to its citizens. "Janus House" must be demolished. And if it harbors anything of value within its walls, and this I highly doubt, then that property must be rightfully seized by the town and sold as recompense for Mount Airy's long-standing troubles with Roman Janus. And if that man objects, then he should be brought to task for the obvious disregard in which he holds our community.

Too long has Janus presented his mummery and charlatanism as practices for which we should be thankful to him – let him keep his "ghosts" and "spirits" to himself, and allow decent people to continue their lives unbesmirched by his brand of "service." And if he has truly abandoned his property, then let it be torn down and bring beauty and tranquility back to our landscape.

Sincerely,

Franklin Parton III

From *The Mount Airy Eagle*
Late Edition - Friday, October 31

...and is my custom, I found myself walking the grounds on Christmas Eve, thinking of Holidays past and the joy that was ours every Christmas morning as children. It seems so long ago, but, of course, it was but a few years ago.

As I passed by Janus House – you know it's deserted, dear Per, don't you? – I was reminded of a tale that Da once told us on a wintry Christmas Eve, one that concerned the sprawling mansion's former owner...or does he in fact still own it? Anyway, it went something like this.

Sgt. Janus was called to the house of an old miser who lived on the outskirts of some little town somewhere, as the skinflint was supposedly troubled with ghosts.

"You of course remember the story of another, ahh, elderly gentleman visited by spirits at this same time of year?' he asked the codger.

"The man passed his rheumy eyes over the famous Spirit-Breaker and coughed. 'Just get on with it, young man,' he spat. 'I'm paying you to clear this house of what ails it, not remind me of musty old tales of fiction.'

"Janus smiled and turned to his task. After searching the entire house he came to the conclusion that the man was not being visited by the dead, but rather by a few very living rodents. This he told the gentleman and waited for the explosion of denial that was sure to come. But none did. The old man simply stared at the sergeant and then exhaled slowly.

"'Then what am I to do of it?' asked the miser.

"'My suggestion would be to bedevil this house's rats no more and move along to your final destination,' replied Janus with a twinkle in his eye.

"And with that the old man vanished in a puff of ancient cigar smoke and a jingle of dusty coins. Sgt. Janus made for the door, his work done. Save for paying his clients, of course.

"A piece of cheese, good and stout, left by the wainscoting and he was off. The next day, Christmas, the man's family found his empty shell of a body in the master bedroom, a few crumbs of cheese littered here and there on the carpet, and, strangely, the clear tracks of hooves on the roof.

"Well, Per, let me burden you no more with old wives' tales and allow me to wish you the very best of the Season and to your husband and my dear nieces.

"Oh, and by the by, I also thought I saw a light on in a window of Janus House, but when I looked again there was none. I wonder what that could possibly mean...?"

Excerpt from a letter by Master James Carlson of Mount Airy to his older sister, Perchance.

Chapter I
DIG DEEP THE WELL

I suppose it should have come as no surprise when Anthony, the boy who lived over our general store with his parents, came to fetch me.

Wild-eyed, flushed with excitement, he begged me to come and see "the most incredible thing" in the town square. How does one refuse an invitation like that? Since I'd returned from university over four months ago, I'd been lying around the house listening to jazz on the phonograph and not much more; now it was October 15 and the people of Canal Chichester most sincerely wanted to know what I was going to do with the rest of my life.

I admit I did, too. At least if I'd found a calling I could get them to stop pestering me, bringing every last bit of this and that to my attention, hoping to spur my interest and spark a career. Anthony's insistence to follow him was just the latest in a long string of subtle and not-so-subtle hints to "get on with it." So, I followed. It's a small town; word would have gotten 'round swiftly if I'd refused the invitation, ardent as it was.

Upon arriving in the square, the boy led me over to a small group of people who'd gathered around something or someone at a small table. The table had been set up with other small tables in the spring as a kind of nod to a Parisian café type of thing, but the lack of people in Canal Chichester who were the kind to waste their time sitting around sipping exotic coffees in town squares more or less put the kibosh on such an idea. I thought it was rather keen, myself.

Anyway, the crowd sort of parted when I arrived and revealed a woman sitting at the table. A woman dressed all in black. I was immediately intrigued.

Moving closer to the strange yet alluring apparition, I saw that what I thought was black was really the deepest of midnight blues. Her dress seemed to soak up the light, but here and there I caught a shimmer of blue highlight along her appealing figure. I also noticed she wore no shoes. Her feet were dirty. Her long, raven-black hair was not.

Something compelled me to step around in front of her, and so I did. Looking over her shoulders I saw that the townspeople had begun to disperse, as if my presence somehow assured them that all was well and I had the situation covered. Maybe I did. Surprised at my boldness – I had no reputation as a rake, not yet – I pulled out the chair opposite the woman and sat down in it. She looked up at me, not in surprise, but with a question on her face, in her eyes. Her eyes were like...metal. Yes, gun-metal *and* crystal. Icy, yet with a kind of otherworldly *movement* behind them. I reasoned that many, many men had looked into those eyes and seen their doom.

At that moment, I was determined not to be one of them.

"Hello," she offered in a calm, controlled voice. "Thank you for joining me. Please, where am I?"

I caught the scent of lavender from her. I have never cared for lavender – my mother, in life, wielded it like a sword – but on this woman it seemed wholly natural and not off-putting. There was also some other scent. Elusive. My brain wanted to say, well, "brimstone," but my brain often speaks unbidden and, too often, foolishly.

"You don't know?" I asked her. "You mean to say that you're not sure where you are?"

"Not only not sure," she replied, "but completely uncertain. If you don't wish to tell me, I will ask the next person I encounter." Without further adieu, she got up from the table in one sleek, smooth movement and on her bare feet before I knew what had happened.

The woman turned from me and began walking away. I got up, knocking my chair over in my haste and jogged after her. "Wait, wait..." I implored, unsure of what was transpiring.

She stopped and wheeled around to face me, yet her eyes did not meet mine. They revolved around the square, several times. Finally, they paused, unfocused. Then, she looked right at me.

"Come," she said, as she clasped my arm with one firm hand. "I have some work for you."

Why, oh why, was my life defined only by people telling me to follow them to employment?

Like a sheep, I followed.

She left the town square and headed down a street that ran along the edge of a string of commercial buildings. Soon, we were walking among the homes of the town's more prominent citizens, a fact illustrated by the houses' grand facades and lustrous lawns. She finally spoke again, asking me where she was.

"This is Canal Chichester," I told her, hoping I didn't sound too patronizing.

"I don't know where that is," she said, "or who I am."

The woman said it matter-of-factly, as if it didn't worry her too overly much, as if it were a minor thing to be addressed at a later time. She glided along the uneven road with purpose and direction, sure in where she was headed though unsure of her own identity. I probably should have stopped her and pressed her to think harder on who she was, but I didn't. I got the impression that she wasn't the sort you interfered with when she was on a tear.

But the rogue in me won out and I suggested that perhaps she would benefit more greatly from attacking the problem of her lost name and place of origin rather than from a walking tour of our town. "Names are often overvalued," she tossed back at me over her shoulder. "Then again, they also may hold immense power. I should be very interested to learn mine once I have done my duty here."

We trudged 'cross streets and lanes, moving further from the town square and into the outlying neighborhoods. Musing on whatever my lady's "duty" could be, I observed the sway of her carriage as we did so, not as a letch or a cad would, but in the hopes that I might be somehow mesmerized by the motion and enter into an oracular state to divine the woman's identity. No such luck.

"Here," she suddenly announced and stopped. I looked up from my reverie to see that we were on the corner of a lonely property, at the far back end of its rear yard and looking up at a large house that sat some distance from us. "This is the spot. There is a spirit here."

Now, I'm not one to cast aspersions, but when a strange woman arrives in your little town, amnesic and bare-footed, and then proclaims that someone's backyard harbors ghosts, well, it's all a little hard to swallow. But, there was something about her that took the harsh, sarcastic words from my mouth and dashed them on the ground.

The woman *believed* what she said.

I looked at the property again and realized that I knew it; coming in from the backside of it had thrown me off my bearings. I'm horrible at estimating distances simply by looking at them, but I'd guessed the yard to be able to contain at least ten houses the size of the one that fronted the property. It all belonged to a Mrs. Grandy, a woman who, to my memory, had always been old.

I remembered that the venerable Mrs. Grandy was a recluse, someone rarely seen and not often heard. By the time I was old enough to toddle out to play with the other children, she was something of a quiet legend in Canal Chichester. Seems that many years ago her beloved husband had left her, just up and walked off one day, and gossip told how she began to cut her ties with the world and keep to herself. One time, when we children were playing in her yard, not far from the spot where I was standing, I looked up to see her watching us play. She glowered and told us to move along; I had the feeling that she was not always a curmudgeon.

"Look here," suggested my companion. She gestured towards the ground. Her finger pointed at a sinkhole.

At least, I believed it was a sinkhole at that moment. The ground had slumped inward, creating an unhealthy-looking depression. I strained my eyes to determine exactly how deep the hole was, for the day was receding and the sun beginning to set.

"Do you know what this is?" the woman asked me. I shook my head in the negative, and then, to my surprise, she continued.

"This," she began, "is a well. A very old and deep one. It is a long-standing practice for some people to poison a well, and fill it full of detritus – furniture, crates, bottles…garbage, essentially. Then, the rest of the space is filled with soil and the outer well structure removed. When they are done, normally, it is as if the well was never there.

"But, too often, the garbage settles, as does the soil, and the wells are once again exposed. I believe that's what's happening here."

"That's all fine and dandy of a tale," I told her, perhaps a bit too sarcastically, "but what of it? Why did you come to this place?"

She looked at me curiously, as if she was seeing me for the first time, as if she hadn't really seen me at all before that moment. Then, she sighed.

"I'm afraid I don't know your name, Mister…?"

I told her my name was Joshua Hargreaves, which might shock anyone who knows me. I answer to many monikers: Josh, Harry, Greaves, even J.H., but almost never my true, full name. It's not a bad one, as far as names go, it's just that no one ever really bothered to call me that. But I had named myself properly to this woman. Why, I am not sure. Call it an overwhelming compulsion, a phenomenon that seemed to overtake me where this woman was concerned.

"And you are?" I added, hopeful.

"Still don't know," she responded. "But I do know that I'm needed here. There is a very angry spirit that inhabits this well.

"And I need you to dig it up for me."

Let me stop right here and address something. The subject of ghosts, to be specific.

I think it's a fascinating subject; perhaps even, when one considers it in a particular light, a terrifying one. But I don't fully subscribe to the theories behind the subject and I'm not sure it's important that I do. Besides a few old tales told to me as a child and the odd, occasional mention by a frightened housewife alone in her house waiting for her husband, I scarce gave spirits much credit.

Before being asked to dig one up, that is. That was an entirely new wrinkle for me.

I looked up at the house, expecting old Mrs. Grandy to appear at any moment, scowling and disapproving. Maybe she'd yell at us to leave her property. I suppose I wouldn't have blamed her if she did. I figured it was only a matter of time before she noticed us poking around at her forgotten, buried well. I wasn't looking forward to it.

"I haven't a shovel," I told the woman. It sounded hollow and pathetic coming out of my mouth. I felt my cheeks heat up, but I have no idea why; this person was not my mother, my sister or, God forbid, my wife.

She pointed silently at a small shed on the property, roughly a stone's throw from where we were standing. I wondered why I hadn't noticed it before. Looking once again at the back of the house, I trotted over to the shed and from within it retrieved a suitable shovel.

Rejoining the woman – damnably annoying to not have something to call her! – I asked her what the plan of action was to be.

"Just the top off it," she said. "Perhaps just the first four or five inches or so. That ought to be enough."

"Enough" for what exactly I didn't know, but there was still something quixotically compelling about her that urged me forward – and made me bite my tongue to keep all my questions from spilling out. Instead, I removed my coat, laid it on the ground next to the depression, stepped gingerly down into it and dug.

The ground within the old well's circumference seemed solid enough, but here and there I got the impression that it wanted to give way. I conjured up visions in my mind of falling through the soil and disappearing beneath it, forever to be lost to the outside world. The digging was easy enough and, within a half-hour, I had removed the top five inches of dirt from the area.

When finished, I looked up at the woman. She wasn't looking at me, though, but at the setting sun. I held my tongue again and climbed back up to her level; once there I sat down a good two yards from the depression. The woman finally looked at me.

"Thank you," she said, matter-of-factly. "Now, we wait."

So, while the sun set and darkness crawled over the landscape, we waited.

Someone was calling my name. I realized in a rush of sensations that I had fallen asleep. Opening my eyes, I saw my companion standing resolutely at the edge of the hole; she had draped my coat over her shoulders and flipped the collar up. It made her look a little like a military man.

Across from her, over the hole, suffused with a queer light, was a man.

I rubbed at my eyes – you know, like someone who cannot believe their own eyes is supposed to do. I looked again.

It wasn't a man, as I first thought. It was more like the…the absence of a man. A man-shaped cut-out through which I was looking. I couldn't comprehend it; it hurt my eyes. Then, its edges blurred and wavered, like the rays of heat on a blistering day will distort the landscape. It hovered above the area that I had dug up, wafting as if in a breeze that the rest of us could not feel.

The woman was talking to…*it*.

"Who are you? What is your name?" she asked plainly. "What is your business here? I…I command you to tell me."

The hesitation in her voice surprised me. Since I had met her, she sounded for all the world like a general, someone who felt quite comfortable being in charge. But at that moment, she sounded unsure. It filled me with dread for some reason.

The wavering enigma said nothing in reply. My companion then did the most puzzling thing; she lifted up one arm towards the thing, as if to show it something in her hand. As far as I could see, she held nothing.

The woman looked at her hand. Her brows knitted in confusion for a quick moment, and then she quickly put her arm down, almost embarrassedly.

The thing over the hole faded away completely. I drew in a breath to heave a relieved sigh, but it instead exploded from my mouth when the woman was suddenly lifted into the air and thrown violently across the yard.

I sprung up with a start and leaped over to where she landed on the grass. I expected her to be unconscious when I bent over her, but she was already stirring and, to my amazement, sat up and smoothed her dress back down over her long, bare legs.

"Are you all right?" I queried breathlessly. She would have broken bones, assuredly.

"Yes," she returned. A strange, almost-smile played around her full lips. "That was exhilarating."

Perhaps university had simply not prepared me for anything resembling the likes of this person. I had no idea who she was, what her own business was in seeking out a spirit in an old woman's backyard, or how she survived such a tumble, but I could not suppress my growing admiration for the woman – fool that she was.

Before she or I could say much else to each other, an odd sound came from the direction of the buried well. We both looked up to witness yet another incredible occurrence.

From below it, a shape pierced the turned up soil of the depression. It grew in size until we could make out its angular construction: a broken, rotted chair. The chair, freed from the dirt, turned of its own accord and then came flying at us.

With a cry of alarm, the woman shoved me away from her and in the nick of time; the ancient piece of furniture crashed down between us and shattered into slimy bits of wood and rotted upholstery. I lay there stunned, my senses as shattered as the chair itself.

"A strong spirit, indeed!" she yelped. "And an angry one! On your toes, Joshua!"

She leapt to her feet and dashed towards the old well. I was climbing hurriedly to a standing position when I looked up to see a glinting mass rise up from the dirt: bottles.

The glass containers shot towards the woman as if projectiles.

Reacting and not thinking, I ran and then jumped with all my speed and might and caught her around the waist. We tumbled to the ground together as the bottles rained down upon the spot we'd just vacated, showering it with sharp, pointed shards of glass.

"Enough of this," said the woman, tersely. Disentangling herself from me and regaining her feet, she swung around in an arc, taking in our entire, immediate surroundings. The darkness hung on everything like a shroud, deep and impenetrable. The air suddenly grew chilly, then downright frigid. I saw my breath before my eyes.

"Spirit!" she shouted, putting some fire behind it. I thought for sure that this would bring Mrs. Grandy and any neighbors in the area – though perhaps we were far enough on the outskirts of town to escape notice from others.

"Spirit, hear me! Talk to me! I cannot allow this to go *any* further, but I *will* parlay if you choose to do so! Otherwise, I will dispel you. Do *not* underestimate me, oh spirit!"

The woman was magnificent. Yes, I admit it; she wasn't exactly the breed of female one brings home to Mother, but, in all, she possessed a charisma and an inner strength I thought reserved only for the male of the species. Call me Neanderthal, I guess.

The air grew colder, if that was possible. A quiet fell about the area; no insects could be heard, nothing. Silent as the, well, tomb, I suppose.

There was some sort of racket then, a far-off clacking noise that seemed to come closer. I could not pinpoint its origin, but looked all around us for its source. Finally, I was certain that it issued from the hole.

Sure enough, the soil parted and a broken crate, jagged and pointed, rose up into the air and hovered there. I could see nothing that would be holding it in place. Just the still, cold air surrounded it. By itself, remarkably, it appeared wholly evil and destructive.

The crate's broken slats turned slowly to point themselves at my lovely companion. I saw a muscle in her long, white neck tense; she was prepared for anything, obviously.

For my part, I knew in my sickened heart that at any second, the object would launch itself at her with all the power of Hell behind it.

9

I heard the crunch of a twig or some such, and peered across the lawn to see a woman standing off a distance. She had come from the house, apparently. It was old Mrs. Grandy.

I felt...relieved? Exhausted? Happy? I don't know what to call it, but some of the tension of the day and evening fled from me when I saw the old woman's arrival. Why? I'm afraid I must repeat myself again: I do not know.

My mystery companion simply looked over at Mrs. Grandy, calm and apparently serene. "Ah," she said, "I see that there are *two* spirits here."

Something hit me hard on the backside and it took a moment to impact my brain that I had suddenly sat down on the ground. Then I was frozen.

Memory flooded through me, everything I had ever heard or known about the old woman. Could it be true? Had she...passed on, without anyone being the wiser? And if so, when? And even more amazingly, why did I immediately accept the word of a stranger that a woman I had known all my life was now standing in front of me as a ghost?

"How?" I croaked. My tongue felt like a bag of pebbles, my mouth dry, arid.

My companion looked at me sympathetically. "Brushing up against the spirit world is not an easy thing for anyone to do, Joshua. Even for such as myself. I understand your reluctance to accept—"

"No! No!" I protested through gritted teeth. "I...I believe you! Oh, God, I believe you...poor Mrs. Grandy. Poor, old Mrs. Grandy, all alone, she..."

Lightning struck me. Realization animated my frame.

"...and her husband!"

The crate that held fast in mid-air over the old well fell heavily to the ground. It sank in a bit, but then simply sat there, as if abandoned.

"Yes," said the woman. "I suspect that her husband," she gestured broadly towards the crate, "fell into this old well years ago, and perished there. Someone then, most likely, covered it over once more, not knowing it was his resting place. He must be sorely angered by now, after years of neglect and loneliness."

The old woman's shade moved closer. It was an amazing thing, how solid she appeared to my eyes. I presumed that many had seen her over the years and assumed they saw the living Mrs. Grandy... unaware that she had passed on.

"Oh, oh," said my lady. She clutched at her mid-section. "I feel waves of desperate loneliness from her. Oh, but the sensation is a strong one. Almost as strong as the ire that rolls off the spirit of her husband.

"Joshua, let us stand back a little way and observe."

She reached out a hand and I reached up to take it. It was cool against my own digits and both soft and sturdy. There was a small jolt or charge that seemed to pass between us, but I chalked it up to the dry air of autumn that hung over everything. The two of us stood closely together and watched the unfolding scene, silently.

The specter of Mrs. Grandy came even closer and passed before us, heading towards the old, slumped-in well. Again, I marveled at her seeming solid appearance. She had an odd look on her face; not the scowl I was used to seeing, but something else, something less stern.

Then, before my gaze, the old woman wavered in the air not unlike the form of the man when I first saw it, over the hole. The particles of light that were Mrs. Grandy broke apart, one-by-one, and then dissipated into the night. Beside me, my lady spoke.

"Go thee to thy rest, oh shades. Thou hast served well in life, now take thy reward..."

A rush of emotion overtook me. Then, as suddenly as it came, it went.

The air lightened, and then grew warmer again. I stepped forward, forgetting that I held my companion's hand in mine. Looking back at her, I felt her fingers release, allowing me to continue on my way.

I approached the old well. The crate had sunk back into it and disappeared from sight. Someone would have quite a chore ahead of them, I thought. This well, this grave, would have to be sealed forever. Against my will, I felt my face crack into a relieved smile.

In the very early morning, I found our chief of police and told him what I had discovered the night before. Oh, yes, there were items of information that I obscured or changed to protect the innocent – namely me – and at first, he focused more on the sad facts of the matter than the holes in my story. Years of being the town oddball, I guess, worked in my favor that time.

A coterie of women from the town made their way into the house and opened it up for the first time in, oh, who knows how many years? Yes, to their surprise they found the skeleton of poor Mrs. Grandy laid out comfortably on a bed in an upstairs room, surrounded by photos of her husband. It had been there for quite some time they said.

The Canal Chichester blacksmith and a carpenter who lived nearby came over and worked on the well. Young Anthony asked to help, but they ordered him to stand to one side and only watch the proceedings. There was much discussion about whether or not to dig down into the area and recover the remains of Mr. Grandy, but our mayor argued strongly that not only would it be dangerous to do so, there were perhaps far worse final resting places. Somehow, he announced, it felt right to leave him there.

And so they did. I didn't issue my own opinion on the subject. I soon found that there was to be far more serious issues on which to speak.

The circuit judge arrived the next morning and he was a surly lot. The Right Honorable Gayten Holding reminded me of a pot roast that had been left in the oven too long, all dried up and of little benefit to anyone. Still, I suppose there were far worse judges who we might have been saddled with for what the mayor kept referring to as a "special hearing."

When Judge Holding was brought up to date on the situation,

I was told by someone who was present that he'd made a sour face after being informed the case revolved around two women, one deceased and one very much alive. So much for impartiality and fairness; we allegedly live in a new, enlightened age, yet some of us still cling to our old prejudices. We would also discover that that very conundrum would rear its ugly head during the hearing.

The dark lady was brought into the room that the chief and the mayor had set up as a temporary court in the back of the post office; it seemed to be the right place, all official and whatnot. I pushed my way up to the front of the audience – yes, just about all of Canal Chichester turned out for the party – and wrangled a seat. All eyes turned to view the stunning woman as she entered into the three-ring circus of our little hastily-assembled court.

There was a *magnetism* about her that I had not previously considered, or at least not consciously. This effect pulled at us all, but as I fought off its advances on my senses I was somewhat surprised to find that it was not only the men present who clearly admired my lady – the women of the town were also under her spell. Curiouser and curiouser.

For her part, the lady did not seem to notice her admirers. Her dark eyes were drifting back and forth between Judge Holding and the other assembled officials of our little town. She betrayed no emotion whatsoever.

"I'm told that you have given no name for yourself to this court," said the judge, frowning through his unkempt and yellowing mustache. "Are you an amnesiac, my good woman?"

"For the moment, yes," she replied. Someone tittered in the crowd and I silently cast a point in her column. Holding was an ass and needed to be taken down a peg or two whenever the opportunity presented itself.

"Well," sighed His Honor, "who will represent you? Surely not yourself?" The disdain dripped off of him.

My lady drew herself up to her full height; again I was struck by the almost-military bearing she possessed. "I am quite capable of speaking for myself, thank you – but, I must ask whether or not this

13

is truly just a hearing or if I am literally on trial for something?" She waggled the handcuffs which adorned her wrists. I bit down on my tongue at the outrage of it all.

Holding leaned forward on his chair behind the crates that had been stacked up to form an erstwhile judge's bench. His beady little eyes flashed.

"Now see here, my dear – you are being held while we look into the matter of the death of a citizen of this town. These proceedings are whatever we say they are, nothing more and nothing less.

"Now, I ask again: who will represent you?"

It's always quite nice to know that you can still surprise yourself and the people around you at the same time and with the same surprising statement at the drop of a hat.

"That would be me, Your Honor," I called from my chair.

It was all fairly unorthodox, but after a bit of haggling over my utter lack of experience with lawyering and the law and a few choice commendations from townsfolk who knew me as a "gentlemen and a scholar" – and with no objection from my would-be client – I was sworn in as the official representative of "Miss Mary Noname."

We began with a dry recitation of the lives of Mr. and Mrs. Grandy and their untimely demises by the chief of police; I nearly fell asleep. Ah, what a wonderful beginning for my career as a solicitor. Still, everyone there had to admit that at least I was finally *doing something*.

"Now," spat Holding, most likely bored himself, "we know everything there is to know about these people and their lives and their deaths. What is *your* part in all this, my good woman?"

"I'll handle this," I told my lady before she could speak. I threw in a little wink at her and I'm quite certain she threw back a slight smile. Of course, it could have been a delayed reaction from the jail food, too.

"And so you see, Judge Holding, sir…"

Basking in my oratory skills, I imagined the thrilling impact I was having on the court. "…this dear lady had never been seen in Canal Chichester before Wednesday. It is my, err, conjecture? Yes, my *conjecture* that she had absolutely nothing whatsoever to do with the sad deaths of the Grandys and to hold her in this manner is a horrible miscarriage of justice."

The sound of nervous applause reached my ears from somewhere behind me. I turned to face Harding squarely, but regretted doing so immediately. He not only looked fit to be tied, but with a good, stout length of chain in addition to rope.

"Young man!" he bellowed. "That's all very fine, but *what is this woman's part in the events of the evening of the day before yesterday?*"

I admit that I had hoped to avoid speaking on those events, but realized then and there that it was unavoidable. I took a deep breath, exhaled and opened my mouth to issue some sort of explanation. What it would be, exactly, I had no real idea.

A cool hand on my shoulder sent a charge through me. I did not need to turn to see who it was; my lady had arisen to interrupt my inevitable trippings of the tongue.

"I will explain to the court, Joshua," she said, taking me in appraisingly with her deeply strange eyes. "You have done a superb job of it, but only I may tell the next part of the story."

"This is highly unusual," harrumphed Holding.

My lady smiled. "I'm afraid that from your point of view, then, it may yet become even more unusual."

The judge sat forward again, frowning and squinting. "Whatever do you mean?"

"I lay to rest the spirits of these Grandys that night," the dark lady explained. "They were in torment, being separated by death, but they are together again now, and at peace and rest."

Judge Holding blinked once, then twice, but his expression remained neutral. There was a pause, the likes of which I did not care for. I was prepared to jump into the breach – God only knew what I would have said – but Holding finally broke the silence.

"You must think us backwards fools," he said menacingly. "We are not so *modern* hereabout that we have completely forgotten the old ways, but to come here before me and ask this court to swallow such a tale…"

My lady set her jaw and narrowed her eyes. I imagined a miniature storm cloud to have begun to form over her head, with lightning and all.

"Then you ignore what is right in front of you, *sir*. What is all around you."

Holding's face darkened at her words. "See here – what do you mean by that, my dear woman?"

"Just this," she returned, icily. "That spirits of the dead are everywhere. And their numbers on this plane are growing.

"There is, in fact, one here, in this room, at this moment."

Upon hearing her words it was as if the entire room had become frozen in ice, or stuck in time itself. Then, slowly, as would be expected of anyone who counted himself among the living, many of us looked cautiously, then nervously, around the room.

The dark lady stood like a lightning rod in the middle of the silent tempest, her expression stony and eyes locked upon the judge. Perhaps to his credit, he did not peer from side to side looking for ghosts, but locked his own eyes upon that of the accused.

I quickly reminded myself that my "client" was *not* accused of anything, really.

"Judge, if I may," I interjected, "what has this woman been officially charged with? We seem to be heading off the path here – either formally accuse her of some crime or let her go."

I felt bold, but I could also feel my lady's eyes turn onto me and burn through me. She wanted to continue to speak on the new theme that had gripped the court. I deferred to her, not knowing what else to do in the absence of a retort from Holding.

"This spirit is in anguish," she said, plainly, as if discussing the weather. "This…man, yes, a man, is not sure of where he is. He is not sure of what has happened to him, and he cannot seem to move on from this place. He is in torment because of these questions. I would venture to say that his torment has translated into events here in this building that have confounded people who have witnessed them.

"In some ways, this spirit resembles those of Mr. and Mrs. Grandy. I wonder if this town has a deeper problem that holds the dead here…"

A short, stout woman suddenly pushed her way to the front of the audience and raised a chubby finger to point at the dark lady.

"Aye, she speaks the truth!" the woman bellowed. "I seen 'em and heard 'em here! Been cleanin' this building for sev'een years now and always wondered what it was the bedeviled it!"

Holding's face flushed crimson and he sucked air in and out of his mouth. His eyes threatened to pop out of his skull, so large had they grown in their sockets.

"You be quiet there!" he admonished the cleaning lady. Banging his gavel on his desk he called for order in the court, though he had seemed to have little control over such.

"Let her talk!" demanded the stout woman. "I wan' to hear 'bout the spooks!"

My dark lady snatched at the momentum in the room and, without waiting for permission, forged ahead. Good for her!

"This man was some sort of…official in life. A man of standing and significance. He had an admiration for the law and for justice, but too often believed he did not serve either to the best of his abilities…he was a sad gentleman. With few friends and fewer lovers."

A loud murmur whipped up in the room and buzzed throughout. I fully expected Judge Holding to begin banging his gavel again, but after I had taken a few steps forward to get a better look at him – people had stepped out into the empty space before the bench – I was amazed at what I saw.

The man was silent, staring at the accused with a wash of confusion over his entire face. His bottom lip quivered, then his whole mouth moved as if to speak, though no words issued forth. He seemed to be stuck, like a skipping phonograph record or the sputtering engine of a feckless motorcar.

Then, at last, Holding gained his tongue.

"You say…you say…my dear woman…that this man, he is… in *torment*?"

We were in deep now. Like the well on the Grandy's property, deep and full of portent, the room and its situation opened up like a maw.

The dark woman left her spot before the judge's bench and approached it. She set one foot in front of the other with assured grace and dignity, and it occurred to me once again, with a kind of military bearing. No one moved to stop her. It was as if a tether existed between her and Holding and an unseen hand was taking up the slack, reeling them in together.

"This reminds me of something," said a voice at my side. I swiveled my head around to take the chief of police. He was pondering something. For some unknown reason, I gave him my attention, despite my client approaching the bench without me to guide her.

"What would that be, Chief?" I asked him, curious.

He stroked his chin, gazing at the dark lady. "Reminds me of that one fellow, you know the one, the one that looks into this sort of thing."

"What sort of 'thing,' Chief?"

His eyes crinkled at their outer edges as he held back what I assumed to be a bit of mirth – or embarrassment.

"Well, spooks and such, if you don't mind my saying." He looked over at the mayor, who had sidled up to us, apparently loathe to be absent from our little tête-à-tête. "You know who I mean, don't you, Barney? He was from here, wasn't he?"

Our honorable mayor nodded solemnly, spoke.

"You mean Janus, of course."

The speaking of that name – one I don't believe I heard before that day – caused a reaction in my lady. Her face swung around to us in a halo of raven tresses, her eyes wide and impatient. A tiny barb of, well, *fear*, I guess, niggled at me.

"What did you say?" she inquired. Her hearing was quite excellent, apparently.

"I said—" responded the mayor, but was cut short by Holding's gavel. You would have thought a rifle had been unloaded right there in the court.

"Never mind that! You, woman! Tell me of this—this—*spirit!*"

The lady placed her long, cool hands on the edge of his desk, her prominent chin almost touching it, and looked up at the judge. "What would you have me tell you of it?"

Holding blinked, gulped several times, then answered in a quiet voice that belied his previous tone. He fussed with the left sleeve of his dark coat. A vein throbbed on his forehead.

"Can you…see him? What does he look like?"

From her perfect lips issued forth a description of whatever – whoever – she allegedly saw in that room.

"He is of medium height and build, but carries himself taller, full of his work and the manner in which he executes it. His style of dress is to cloak himself in warm colors, so as to off-put the coldness he must too often dispense as part of his duties. His hair is almost white and his face is clean of whiskers. His eyes are…well, they are violet."

Holding paled at the words. He sat back in his chair, almost removing himself from our sight. He began to speak after a moment, his voice issuing forth not unlike an invisible spirit himself.

"I—I know him," he said in a hushed tone. I had to strain my ears a bit to hear him. "He was—*is* my friend. Judge Geoffrey Bond. 'My word is my bond,' he would quite often say…"

"He died several years ago," added the dark lady. "Alone and penniless."

"Yes," Holding replied. "He would give his money away to almost anyone who asked for it. I told him more than once how foolish it was, but he insisted that it was in direct balance to the cases in which he ruled more from politics than justice. He was my mentor, my…symbol of all that was intended when our system of law and order was established.

"And…I have failed him."

With that Holding let out a loud grunt and then an even louder moan. Both were infused with a heady dollop of evident pain.

I leapt up to the bench to ascertain what had happened, but my lady won that race and pushed in before me. We saw Judge Holding slack in his chair, grasping at his arm with a grip like a steel trap, his mouth set in a rictus of anguish.

"Heart attack," announced my lady as she loosened the man's collar and felt around for a pulse at his neck and then at his wrist. She handled the actions with proficiency; one might have believed she was a nurse the way she deftly checked the man's vital signs. Despite, this, I tore my eyes from the scene and turned to yell for a doctor.

"Too late for that, Joshua," came the words I feared to hear. "But not for another form of aid."

Within seconds, we had the judge on the floor of that impromptu courtroom, arms and legs akimbo at the direction of the accused. We ringed around the man's prostate form; myself, the chief, the mayor, the bailiff and two members of the town council as witnesses.

Witnesses to *what* exactly I could not know at the moment.

My lady spread her skirts, sat down right on the floor above the judge's head and took his temples in her fingers. His skin had already begun to lose its color. I bit my lip, confused and adrift. Remarkably, no one in the circle protested her actions; perhaps Holding's egregious reputation silenced any objections.

Or perhaps everyone present was simply as curious as myself as to what would come next.

"Judge Holding, come forth!" insisted the woman, cradling the man's head in her hands. She leaned down, setting her face above his, merely inches from it. I swear she was breathing directly into his mouth. The religious implications of her choice of words I will not dissect here; suffice to say I could feel the others squirm an iota or so when they heard them.

"Can—can he *speak*?" asked the bailiff.

My lady replied without looking up at the questioner. "Of course not, you silly man; he's *dead*."

Something started to issue from between Holding's rapidly-bluing lips.

A tendril of pale smoke or steam wafted upwards and into my lady's features. She did not blink. She did not cough. She held fast and allowed the vaporous excursion to spread out and envelop her entire head.

"Yes, yes," she whispered, but not to us. She spoke to…the judge, I presumed.

"Of course; I will tell them. Yes, most certainly. What? Oh, I am happy to inform you that he *is* here. There, you see him? Take his hand – you will depart together. Hmm? I do not know why, but that is in the past now; together you will find Elysium.

"Go. Go thee to thy rest, oh shades. Thou hast served well in life, now take thy reward. And tarry not."

Court was adjourned then and we all turned away to head back to our own dreary lives. Elysium would elude us for at least another day, thankfully.

Holding's body was examined later by a doctor and a massive heart attack was pronounced as the official cause of death. Rather a useless thing to report, I admit, but there you have it anyway.

Canal Chichester went back to its normal, daily existence. A few of us had learned something or other, but we did not rush to speak of whatever that may have been with our neighbors.

The dark woman? She of the long, raven tresses and lavender scent and the ability to break spirits free from their Earthly ties and send them on their way? Cleared of involvement in any murder, mayhem or morbidity, she left the next day. Refused a ride. Refused anything that was offered to her. Wanted to walk.

She left Canal Chichester on foot, as she had, presumably, arrived. Told me she knew where she was headed, but wasn't sure where exactly it was, or what it was called. Said she had business to attend to.

Then she looked at me, touched me on the shoulder and spoke one final word.

"Janus."

As she walked away, I thought of her as a well; a deep, deep well, of which I had only minutely peered into its darkness over the last few days.

I thought I might forget her, eventually, but I was hoping that I might not.

Chapter II
THAT MAN RIGHT THERE

I had barely knocked on the door of the sprawling, shambling old manse when the heavy oaken portal was suddenly thrown open and I was greeted by the sight of she who I had come to see.

"Ah, good," she said, nodding and narrowing her strange cut-glass eyes at me. "Come along."

I had a speech prepared, you see, but all in a rush there didn't seem to be any time for it. I wrote the speech on the train to Mount Airy and tightened it up a bit during the taxi cab ride to what the locals call "Janus House." The speech began, "I humbly offer my services…" and then rambled into various inanities. I was fairly certain my lady had done me a favor by affording me little chance to unspool it.

She slammed the door behind her and darted past me; inside the house I had glimpsed precious little save for dusty curtains and a darkened foyer. I looked around me at the porch I stood upon and at my prey's departing backside. Then, I followed. It's what I do best.

"Do you drive?" she asked me as I caught up to her.

"Passably well," I replied, puzzled.

My lady was still dressed in the dark, midnight-blue vestments she wore when I first met her more than four months ago in my hometown of Canal Chichester, but she had added a topcoat and a few other pieces since then. Overall, the effect gave one the impression that she wasn't quite sure whether to dress herself in feminine fashion or in a more severe style, not unlike a man. In the end, her look settled somewhere in the middle; at least she was wearing shoes, it being late February and all when I found her at Janus House.

"To the garage," she commanded, pointing 'round to the rear of the property. "Joshua? It *is* Joshua, is it not?"

I swelled and puffed myself up a bit in her remembering my name – perhaps my long quest was to have been worthwhile after all. Alas, no more niceties flowed from her, only a headlong pitch towards the garage and her grumbling of what a "damned nuisance" her long, black hair was as she began to tie it back behind her head with a royal blue ribbon she produced from a pocket.

I was determined to begin at last one exchange between us on my own. "Aren't you in the slightest bit interested in why I'm here?" I asked her. "Why I sought you out?"

Seemingly ignoring me – no, she *was* ignoring me – she pulled up in front of a large set of doors that covered what I presumed to be the garage and threw them open. Dust and cobwebs floated in the air between the disturbed portals.

Inside the building lay a marvelous collection of automobiles.

My eyes must have gleamed as I took in the vehicles. There were two Lincolns, a Ford, a Packard and a Caddy. Something about the rust-colored Lincoln appealed to me and I assume it shown on my face for my compatriot jabbed one slender finger at it.

"That's the one then," announced my lady, and she flung open its passenger door and hopped inside. "Let's go, Joshua. We're needed."

I sighed and, after a moment to collect my wits, got the thing started and gave it the gas. Despite the cobwebs that covered it, the auto came swiftly to life and gave me no trouble. I pulled out of the garage and steered it down the drive to the road.

"Where to?"

"The city."

I looked over at her. "Mount Airy?"

"No," she answered, "the *city*. Here is the address." She handed me a scrap of paper with a few manly scribbles on it.

Now beginning to fume a bit, I bit down on the words that desperately wanted to tumble out of my mouth. I wanted to tell her of my adventures in tracking her across several counties after I had made up my mind that there was little in Canal Chichester to hold me down and a world of possibilities in leaving. Some of those possibilities…well, I admit I was loathe to put voice to them at that moment.

"What do I call you?" I shouted above the whipping wind.

It took several minutes for her to reply; I assumed it would be another bout of ignoring me. But, I could see her chewing on her inner thoughts and I gave her the space she needed to give me an answer. I suppose I knew then what it was like to propose marriage to someone and watch them mull over the decision.

"*Janus*, I…I presume."

It was the name of the house in which she had taken up residence, which lead me to believe that even after the time that had gone by since I last saw here, she was still an amnesiac. Was it natural that she had grasped onto a name that intrigued her? She had, after all, followed that name from hearing it in Canal Chichester to a property outside the town of Mount Airy that also bore it.

It was all very strange. And that name rang a bell with me, though at the time I couldn't place where I had heard it before coming to Mount Airy.

"Joshua, I'm growing stronger." Her fingertips grazed the sleeve of my coat.

"I'm glad to know it," I told her, a bit bewildered. "Had you been ill?"

"Do you own a gun?" she asked me, her lips suddenly an inch from my ear.

I flinched at the question and her proximity, both a surprise. "No," I said plainly, "I'm a confirmed coward. I have papers and other documentation."

A tad of shadow fell over us then, an odd tang in the air that I was moved to dispel, and quickly. I pointed to the dashboard in front of her.

"Probably one in the glove compartment," said I with what I

hoped sounded like a jovial tone. Leaning over to twist the handle of the tiny enclosure, I hit a nasty bump in the road and sprawled into her lap instead. The softness of her skirts welcomed me as well as her heady lavender scent, but embarrassment straightened my spine and I returned to my former upright position, red-faced.

My lady opened the glove compartment herself, seemingly oblivious to the awkward situation, and reached inside. Her hand reappeared clutching a pistol.

With the pistol nestled away in my pocket and a promise to let me handle such things on my traveling companion's lips, we pulled up to the curb in front of a tall, stone edifice. Around us, the city hummed and burbled, as cities will do.

Luck was with us as we had navigated the streets and found the address we sought with little to no difficulty; between my lady's directions and my own small knowledge of the city, we managed to somehow not become lost. Exiting our vehicle, the two of us looked up at the building in tandem and saw a flight of steps leading up to its doors and rather large windows that revealed the hustle and bustle of its inhabitants. Ah, *business* – a stranger to me, let me assure you.

A somewhat hastily-lettered sign propped up in one window read "REALE PICTURES, INC."

We were met just inside the doors by a young woman, businesslike but with a saucy gleam in her eye, I thought. As the pretty little thing appraised me, my lady told her we had an appointment. Chivalrous if not anything, I stepped around my companion and took charge of the situation.

Three men stepped out of an office down the hall and walked briskly up to meet us. Leading the pack was a stout gentleman with a great walrus moustache and pince-nez; the others kept up yet maintained an arm's length behind him.

The walrus looked me and my lady up and down, obviously confused. Who could blame him? I myself had no idea why I was there.

"We had expected a Sergeant *Janus*," he grumbled at me. "That would be *you*, sir?"

I admit I was surprised. Sgt. Janus? I had recently heard the name connected with the military title, but at that bewildering moment I had forgotten when and where. Recovering quickly – I was always light on my feet – I stepped to one side to extend a hand to the woman who accompanied me. Or was *I* accompanying *her*?

"Gentlemen, may I present...ah...*Lady* Janus..."

She did not take my hand but moved past me to extend her own to the walrus. Fairly cheeky, but modern times and all that, I suppose. The stout man took her hand lightly and made a short, quick bow over it. Once again erect, he beetled his brow at my lady and appraised her fully.

"You...speak for him, then? The sergeant?" His inquiry came out less gruff then when addressing me, but still laced with confusion. I sympathized with him.

"Mr. Reale," my lady began, "all that I know is that your message arrived at my home and, seeing as how you requested aid of a specialized sort which is within my purview, I came."

Her home?

The walrus' eyes actually twinkled at her comment. "My dear woman," he snorted, but not in an unkind way, "my name is Herbert Marshman Pettigrew, not Reale. 'Reale Pictures' is the name of my company, a fanciful name chosen at the height of my ardor with the celluloid arts, if I'm to be truthful about it."

"You make moving pictures, then?" I interjected. "For the theaters?"

You would have thought I had said something rather inept. All three men looked at each other and then back at me, as if some sort of bug that had crawled along the carpet and into view. Pettigrew asked my lady who I might be.

"This, gentlemen, is Joshua Hargreaves, my-my...well, *chronicler* of sorts," she offered. "I suppose," she added. With this nugget she fixed me with a gaze that could have fed me for an entire week. Perhaps even two. And then it was gone as quickly as it came.

"This is Mr. Clark and Mr. Gayme," Pettigrew threw over his shoulder. "If you will come with me, Lady Janus, I shall illuminate our problem in the screening room."

The three men turned as one and stamped off back down the hall and towards the office they had vacated to greet us. My companion took my arm and we followed.

"We shall have a talk later," she whispered to me, "about '*Lady Janus*.' I'm not afraid to tell you I don't care much for it."

I smiled at her. "What can I say; I'm only a simple-minded 'chronicler'…"

"Reale Pictures has swiftly become one of the preeminent motion picture studios in the country," announced Mr. Pettigrew as we were offered plush chairs in the room in which we were ushered. "And our films have won numerous awards, as well as a tidy sum at the box office."

Mr. Gayme spoke up. "I am the producer on Mt. Pettigrew's latest production, *A Woman in the City*. We have been filming here on the streets for three weeks, capturing the local flavor, you know. These offices," he gestured around himself, "have served as a temporary headquarters for our production. Mr. Ashton Clark here is our director."

Clark nodded, obviously not a very talkative chap. He looked like a brandied dandy. My lady looked at all three men in succession and then to me.

"I don't understand any of this, Joshua. What do they mean by all of it?"

I was at a loss for words; why was she asking *me*? Still, I stammered out a reply, trying to be helpful, but knowing that all eyes were upon me.

"Well, Lady Janus…" – she caught me with a withering glare – "these gentlemen run a *film company*. They make motion pictures." A blank stare from her. "They're really quite popular now, the picture shows…you know of them, of course." Another blank look. "Um, the, ah, running of a piece of film with, ahh, many images on it, through a-a projector?" I was stymied – hadn't she ever been to a picture show?

Pettigrew cleared his throat, spoke. "My lady, a cellulose-based carrier strip that has been coated with a chemical composition – an emulsion – that is exposed to light, not unlike the still photographs, but producing a series of images. When run all together through a projector they produce the illusion of movement..."

"And what has this to do with me?" she asked, cocking a midnight eyebrow. I believed wholeheartedly, then and there, that the woman had no prior knowledge of what she was being told.

The men all looked sheepishly at each other. Sheepishly!

"Perhaps we should just show her the film, Herbert," Gayme suggested. Pettigrew assented and leaned over to douse the lamp next to his chair. The other two men did the same with more lamps and the room was plunged into darkness. My lady showed absolutely no shock or surprise or concern, as if she was more at home in darkness than in the light.

Came the sound of a switch being manipulated and a fluttering, flickering beam of light appeared and flooded a screen at the far side of the room. Suddenly, flat, moving images emerged from the darkness and danced before our eyes.

We watched as a woman of very apparent low standing approached a restaurant of very apparent high standing, and, after a momentary hesitation and a card that read "She Knew Her Lover Awaited Her Inside..." the woman entered the establishment.

My companion made a small sound beside me, but kept her eyes glued to the screen.

The scene shifted to an interior shot of the restaurant's lobby, occupied by a few people in evening dress. One older man stood just behind an armchair off to one side, staring into space, while another man and his female friend chatted amiably next to the maitre d's stand. Our heroine slunk up to the stand, peering all around her, conscious of her care-worn clothes and unkempt hair.

Not exactly the most engrossing of stories. I had seen better.

Pettigrew's voice rang out in the dark. "Stop! Stop the film!" A rather inane thing to say, really, for it was he who was running the projector.

The images ground to a halt and froze on a long shot of the restaurant's lobby, the players halted in their actions. I was immediately concerned that the film would begin to burn, having being stopped with the hot light of the projector still glowing directly behind it.

"You see there?" pointed Pettigrew at the screen. Gayme jumped up from his chair, put a hand on the walrus' arm.

"See? How could she *see*, Herbert? We've barely told her anything."

Sure that I had wormed my way into an apple core of madness, I heard my lady speak.

"Gentlemen, I thank you for this interesting lesson in these 'pictures' and would be happy to help you, but I simply don't see the trouble for which you have brought me here."

Another voice came to my ears, one that I had not heard before. With a start I realized it was that of Mr. Clark, the gussied-up director of the film.

He approached the screen, staring intently at its frozen tableau. His hand darted out suddenly, well-manicured index finger pointing at one of the players. It was the older man by the chair, off to one side of the scene.

"That man right there," he said softly.

"He wasn't there when we filmed this."

My companion fairly leapt from the Lincoln barely a second after I pulled up to the curb alongside of "La Maison d'Havelock," the restaurant used in the snippet of film we had just viewed.

I bit down on a comment concerning men and their duty to open doors of all kinds for ladies. I was learning in leaps and bounds of just what sort of lady my raven-tressed whirlwind was.

"What do we know?" I asked instead. My lady spun around to skewer me with a look.

"What do you mean?" she asked in turn, fists on hips and flush of face.

Rejoinders filtered through my brain – such as it is – and I threw caution to the wind. "Who is *Sgt.* Janus? Why did you answer a message meant for him? *What* do you hope to accomplish here?"

She stepped up to me, faced me head on. "I don't know," she said quietly, dusky colors swirling in and out of her eyes. "But I do know that I'm needed, in there" – she gestured at the restaurant – "and you will either come with me or you will not."

The dark woman turned and reached for the door to the establishment. I followed, not for the first time and not for the last, and insisted on holding that door for her.

"I know this place – or, rather, its proprietress."

"Do tell, Joshua," she threw over her shoulder as we marched across the lobby and to the maître d stand. Shades of a film I once I saw...

I caught her sleeve and tugged her gently back to me. "Valerie Havelock-Mayer. A very powerful woman who not only owns this restaurant, but most likely the entire block. We must tread lightly here."

A peaceful soul down to my very core and an inveterate non-confrontationist, I implored her with my eyes to stop and think things through. My feeling at that time was to be wary of webs we had no business being caught up in.

"Of course," my lady agreed. "We need only scout the area and determine the exact whereabouts of the intrusive spirit in question, he whom we saw in that 'picture show' of yours. Nothing could be simpler, Joshua."

Setting aside the fact that it was not *my* picture show, it was then that I learned yet another truth about her: my lady was a poor liar. "Simple" was not a word she used with honest intent.

Securing a table – thank goodness we both appeared relatively well-heeled, or at least *she* did – I plunked myself down and looked around at the opulence of our surroundings. The film had not done it justice; La Maison d'Havelock was a bit above my station.

Then, the disturbance I had expected *and* predicted came almost immediately.

The restaurant was filled with patrons that Saturday afternoon, a testament to its reputation and the delightful scents that issued forth from its kitchen and from the plates which adorned the tables. My stomach growled, an embarrassment that proved minor compared to what was to come.

Said patrons were beginning to realize that they were under intense scrutiny from my charming companion. And, understandably, they were not terribly amused by it.

"Lady Janus," I called out loudly. "Why, won't you look at your menu, my dear? Yes, it is a fine establishment, is it not? What will you have?"

"*Don't call me that*," she hissed. "I am looking for our spirit. I am not here to *eat*."

"You're disturbing our fellow diners," I sing-songed to her *sotto voce*. "And besides, isn't it the very point of a spirit that you cannot *see* it?"

She tossed a dagger at me with those eyes of her. "Ridiculous. You should know better than that, after the incident at the well last year. Now, be quiet and allow me to concentrate."

She had a point, but concentration was not to be hers, I'm afraid – the full water glass thrown from an adjoining table onto my lady ended any such effort.

Chaos ensued. A richly-coiffed woman at that table stood up and shrieked, bellowing, "I did not throw that! I did not throw that! Waiter, oh, waiter!" The two men with her looked at each other and then at me, most likely assuming I had something to do with it. My lady wiped the water from her face and stood up so violently that her chair fell back and smacked against the floor behind her.

"You're here all right!" she announced in a strong, commanding voice. "You cannot and will not continue this behavior. I will see you put out of this place!"

In any other circumstance, I might have complimented my companion on her almost-exact precognition of the words which would momentarily be addressed to her.

Food fountained from plates and dishes and bowls like several unruly volcanoes, but not by mortal hands. Women *and* men yelped in surprise and confusion. I saw my new profession sinking like a stone dropped in a pond.

My dark lady sprang from her place at our table and weaved between others as she sought out the spirit that seemed to take a great dislike to her. I tried to follow her visually through the crowd, but lost her as she moved behind a large, potted fern of some exotic variety.

This would become something of a tradition with us.

Suddenly, a voice rang out from the other side of the dining room. To say it had the best qualities of a finely-crafted bell would be an understatement; it split the room like Joshua's trumpet. Ah, the *biblical* Joshua, of course, not yours truly.

Damn and blast it all – it was Valerie Havelock-Mayer herself.

She called for her patrons to calm themselves. Then, pointing with swift and fine precision, she identified my lady and myself.

"There and there," the woman noted us. Tall and strongly-boned, Valerie Mayer-Havelock struck me as a countess, or some other sort of royalty. Her fine figure, dressed in a dark, blood-red evening gown, drew men's stares and woman's envy – even in the midst of the chaos, I could see the reactions among her guests.

"You will not continue this behavior here in my place. I will see you put out this instant."

You see? What did I tell you? Precognition. Astounding.

The woman's rich auburn hair, unadorned by *chapeau*, danced with the quick jerks of her head as she made sure her employees saw us and moved to secure our expulsion from the restaurant.

Before we exited the doors of La Maison d'Havelock – manhandled by overzealous waiters – I made an unfortunate mistake that would haunt us far more than any ghost ever would and for some time to come.

"Come, Lady Janus," I said with what I hoped would sound like money-laden righteous indignation, "let us be gone from this *eatery*."

We were barely out the door when I heard Valerie Havelock-Mayer cry out at our departing backsides.

"*What* did you say?"

33

"Here," said my lady, stabbing a finger at the newspaper on the table before us.

We had removed ourselves to the city's library, a towering structure filled with musty old volumes and cranky attendants. Myself, I was still reeling from Valerie Mayer-Havelock's daggers, the ones that she shot from her eyes as we left her establishment. I assumed we hadn't heard nor seen the last of her. Unfortunately, I was becoming something of a reliable fortune-teller.

"Five years ago, some sort of troubles at that restaurant – Joshua, are you listening?"

Seems there was more than one dagger-shooting female in town. I hastened to attend to my companion's words. She spread out several more of the newspapers we'd been sifting through, acquired from the library's archives, and I peered at them.

"Here a report of a 'break in,'" she said, still pointing, "and here another. That would seem odd, but perhaps not so overall strange. But *here*, look at this…a fire."

I read the article she presented, quickly. "Agreed. They'd been having a spot of difficulties, certainly. And the articles are a bit longer each time; I'm sure Valerie Havelock-Mayer was quite put out by it all. By the way, is all this dusty research part and parcel of your usual method of operation?"

My lady ignored that. "It must have been the spirit at work," she whispered after a moment's reflection. "But why? What is it that upsets it so?"

"I should think simply being *deceased* would be enough to upset anyone," I offered.

Expecting another round of daggers, I was pleasantly surprised to find myself favored with a thoughtful look from my dark lady.

"You bring up a valid point, Joshua," said she. "Some spirits are not aware of their condition. They believe themselves still among the living and are often frustrated at not being able to interact with others as they did in life. This causes strife and with that strife comes spirit phenomena such as poltergeist activity – quite often violent. Again, remember our troubles at the well."

I was about to reply that I was trying to *forget* our "troubles at the well" when all of a sudden something caught my eye on another of the newspapers sitting nearby.

The name "Janus" drew me in like a beacon.

She read the article I indicated, her focus razor-sharp and her concentration complete. My lady drank in the words as if they were water to someone who'd just crossed a desert, so intense, so desperate was her interest in the words before her.

When she had finished, she pushed the newspaper across the table to me and bade me read. As I began to digest the article, my confusion grew.

"'The proprietress of La Maison d'Havelock also welcomed another special guest to sample the fine dishes offered that evening,'" I quoted. "'Sgt. Roman Janus of Mount Airy...'"

I skewered my companion with a pointed look of my own. "That name does seem to pop up, doesn't it?" I said aloud, feeling as if we were beginning to get to the bottom of the matter. "It's not just a coincidence, am I right? Our motion picture men expected this sergeant, Valerie Havelock-Mayer reacted to the name...and...what was it that they said back in Canal Chichester? Janus was...born there?"

Lady Janus sat there, silent, staring off into space in much the same fashion as the ghost on the film. I watched her eyes, those strange dark orbs, as they contemplated the wall next to our work table. The name had triggered something within the woman. At loose ends, I looked back down at the article to escape the awkwardness of the moment.

A phrase caught my eye: "...famous 'spirit-breaker.'"

Who *was* this Sgt. Janus?

"Recall the attire of our spirit."

I nearly jumped out of my skin at the words – my lady was back among the living. When I had recovered, I asked her to clarify her statement.

"Think back to the clothes worn by the ghost on the motion pic-

35

ture," she said. "They were old, weren't they? Out-of-date?"

I searched my memories, shaken though I was by recent developments. I agreed that yes, now that she'd mentioned it, the man looked to be from an earlier era…perhaps from even before the turn of the century.

My lady lit up like a Roman candle, animation filling her frame. She vanished and then returned shortly with a small cart stacked with more newspapers, these appearing to be of an older and mustier condition than that which we'd previously perused. I groaned and rolled up my sleeves.

The game was afoot – again.

As we drove away from the library and with the last of my sneezes from the dust of centuries we'd stirred up, we consolidated our data.

"We know that the restaurant was once a grand theatre," she began, "and that it nearly burned to the ground forty-four years ago."

"Leaving not much more than a shell of structure," I added. "We also now know that someone died in that fire."

"Francis Richard Briefer," she continued, "a very popular stage actor at the time who lived on the premises. The theatre company never rebounded from the loss and the building sat dormant for twenty years – until Mr. Richard Mayer bought it and refashioned it as a restaurant."

I nodded, the picture becoming clearer in my head. "So, we have our ghost and we have our, err, *motive*? The actor is angered that his beloved theatre is gone, yes?"

"Presumably. We have nothing better to go on. I sense that it is the correct conjecture, though."

I believed her. I had no real, concrete reason to do so, but such was the power of my lady's passion for the subject. It almost made me forget all the mystery over Sgt. Janus. Almost.

"And if I'm right," she noted, her eyes boring into the side of my face, "*that* is how we draw the spirit out."

"And 'break' it, eh?" I inquired.

Silence.

Perhaps my tongue has too much a mind of its own. It too often goes off and the rest of me must pay the price for its reckless abandon.

Silence, more damnable silence. Then, words and a soft touch of fingers upon my wrist.

"Joshua." She named me quietly, pausing after doing so.

"I am not completely well yet, but you must *trust* in me…"

I tore my eyes from the road and swung my head around sharply to take her in. I met her eyes, my face hot.

"Where to then, Lady Janus?"

I pulled my cap down over my head and slumped my shoulders; wasn't I supposed to be some sort of roustabout or whatever they call the laborers in a motion picture troupe?

Lady Janus was dressed much as myself, in well-worn work clothes and boots, with a big floppy cap to top off the ensemble. We had to dirty her up a bit more to give her the manly look of a menial worker. Because of that, she appeared even more uncomfortable then I, which provided me a kind of perverse joy, I must admit. Not too much, but there you have it.

My lady had convinced Herbert Pettigrew that he should return to La Maison d'Havelock to film more scenes for his picture, with the addition of myself and my companion as extra hands. It was all very cloak and dagger, but I could see the point behind her plan: we would lure our ghost in by combining the two things which seemed to draw his ire the most, the restaurant and motion pictures.

It made a kind of sense. This Briefer was an actor's actor, a consummate professional who trod the boards and worked his craft to perfection. Sadly, his kind was disappearing behind the bloom of motion pictures – no wonder he was outraged at their flowering.

Pettigrew had arranged everything with Valerie Havelock-Mayer, and we were to enjoy the luxury of having the restaurant to ourselves after it had closed its doors for the evening. The proprietress herself would not be present – thankfully – but our producer promised her that he would require her for another scene to be shot at a later date. Seems that no one can play-act the part of a restaurant owner quite like a real restaurant owner.

My lady and I shuffled around in the background while the real hands set up the motion picture equipment and the actors were prepared by makeup artists for their scene. Several actual restaurant employees, including the maître d, were present, thus our disguises. Ashton Clark, the director, reasoned that he shouldn't waste a perfectly good opportunity to "get a few more feet in the can" and therefore would be using real film in the camera that evening.

My companion slipped away from me in the hubbub and I was left alone with my thoughts.

As I watched the troupe bring together the various elements for filming, I pondered the puzzle of Sgt. Janus. Surely the man, described as a "spirit-breaker," had sensed the ghost when he had visited the establishment several years ago? Was it the reason he had visited? Perhaps Valerie Havelock-Mayer had invited him with that express purpose, to drive out the entity that she herself might have begun to suspect as the source of her troubles.

And, if so, had Janus "broken" the spirit? What did that even mean? I'd heard of flim-flam men before, illusionists and sleight-of-hand tricksters who preyed upon the more gullible amongst us and bilked them of their hard-earned money…was Janus one of those? A spiritualist with ill intent, perhaps? Or a dark Houdini?

But if he were the real thing, a man who somehow could get rid of ghosts, and he came to La Maison d'Havelock to rid it of its vexing spirit, why would he have let it be if he had not succeeded?

The thought chilled me. I sensed somehow this Janus' standing as a respected personage in the community…he might have truly helped people. He might really have been able to vanquish these ghosts. But if so, why was the presumed spirit of Francis Richard Briefer still haunting the restaurant?

Can a spirit return once it had been "broken"? Was Sgt. Janus fallible?

Cold dread gripped me. What was I doing there? Who was Lady Janus and why had I placed myself in her service?

What if she was fallible, too?

I finally spotted my beautiful companion across the room just as the first scene was about to begin.

Some of the clammy feeling that infused me washed away as I gazed at her face below her cap. With her raven tresses shoved up under it and her fine figure nearly obscured by her work clothes disguise, she could almost pass for a man – if a person had not known her previously as the handsome woman she was. I, though, could see the feminine below the male artifice and it provided me with a modicum of calm.

Ashton Clark called for "quiet on the set" and the resounding chitter-chatter of the troupe died down immediately. A half-circle of bright lights set up by the hands bore down on two of the actors who had accompanied us to the restaurant; others of their ilk sat at tables nearby, frozen in tableau and awaiting the call for filming to begin.

My lady peered around the room, her interest quite evidently on more nebulous things.

"Action!" shouted Clark, and the cameraman began to crank his equipment and the actors sprang into life. The duo in front of the camera, the girl from the snippet of film we'd watched – still with care-worn clothes and unkempt hair – and a man in resplendent evening dress acted out a pantomime of misery and love. Damn me, but I found it rather fascinating to witness.

Something niggled in my brain and I looked up suddenly to find my lady staring at me, trying to gain my attention. Having secured it, she pointed around the dining room, silently urging me to keep watch with her. I ashamedly complied.

The scene ended and the director yelled "Cut!" Another scene was prepared with a brief discussion between Clark and his actors, and then the man settled back into his chair and spoke a few words to his cameraman. When he had finished, the director looked over at Lady Janus, one eyebrow cocked in question. She shook her head from side to side in answer and motioned for him to continue with the filming.

No sooner had Clark yelled for action there came a clattering on the other side of the room, near the swinging doors to the kitchen.

"It has begun," I said to myself under my breath. Once again my prediction proved accurate.

My companion stalked off towards the disturbance. I tracked her with my gaze – from behind how like a man she looked.

Suddenly, a large silver serving tray slid off a stack of trays and rocketed like a discus at my lady. It caught her in the midsection and with a soft expulsion of air she fell backwards onto a table.

I yelped in surprise. So, too, did most of the others in the room. They stood up *en masse*.

It was somewhat dark in the great room around the halo of bright motion picture lights. Had I really seen what I thought I saw?

Finding myself moving towards Lady Janus' position, I swung back around to the sound of an unearthly moan; it was as if a great wind blew through the restaurant, howling as it came.

Light filled my eyes, blinding me. I threw up my arms, unable to move. I felt the steely hand of death upon me.

One of the great motion picture lights flew past me and across the room, headed for my lady.

In an instant, my revolver was in my hand and I fired. The lamp's gigantic head exploded in a shower of sparks as it fell to the floor like an immense bird of prey shot out of the sky. It crashed onto the carpet with a resounding release of fury.

"Joshua!" screeched my dark lady as she raced up to me and grabbed me by my rough coat. I thought that it was a gesture of great relief at first, but then felt her violently tug at me to move.

Another of the great lights came down right next to us, missing our persons by mere inches. Screams from the actors and crew almost drowned out the sound of the crashing mechanism.

Then darkness.

It came on all in a hurry. I thought perhaps it was from the absence of the two suicidal lights, but then immediately I knew it was something much more than that. The darkness was inky and deep; a most unnatural fall of shadows.

"Quiet, everyone!" shouted Clark. Inwardly, I praised the man for the quick recovery of his wits. I was not so fortunate. "Miss Janus, what *is* it?" he asked then.

"All of you, reach out to your companions and form yourselves into an unbreakable chain!" my lady hissed. "Quickly! And once you are a chain, then form yourselves into a ball. Do it now!"

I could hear the shuffling of feet and the mewling from many mouths. Hands grasped at me and I realized it was my lady. We drew into each other and grasped hands.

"Look!" I whispered in her ear, not wanting to alarm our troupe further. Trying to orient my lady physically, I hoped she would discern what I was seeing off in the distance.

"Do you remember your positions in the room?" Lady Janus asked of the crowd. "Move towards the lobby as a group. Do not disengage from each other! You will be fine. I will protect you."

I watched as a small ball of light appeared high up, most likely at the level of the ceiling. It grew ever so slightly, bobbling as it I guessed it moved towards us. It glowed with a sickly hue, swampish green and malignant.

"He's coming down to us," said my companion quietly, for my ears only.

"Coming down? From *where*?" I prayed the troupe had reached the lobby.

"From above," came the answer. "From the old theatre."

It did indeed appear to me then that the light reminded me of someone walking down a long flight of steps, perhaps while holding a flashlight or lantern. But there were no more steps, just as there was no more theatre.

"I will face him," whispered my lady. "Let go of me, please, Joshua."

My hands locked on hers by their own accord. She did not remonstrate me for the failing, but merely brushed the backs of my hands with her thumbs, softly, and I released her.

I felt her move away from me, receding warmth in the all-pervading darkness.

41

The ghost-globe continued on its way down to meet us.

"That will be far enough."

I was reminded at that moment of a gunfighter from the Old West, a lone man stepping out into an empty street to act as a bulwark against the advance of his opponent.

My lady stood directly between myself and the sickly light, for it lit her up in silhouette; I could see that she had doffed her cap and her coat. Arms and legs akimbo, she filled me with hope, hope that we would somehow walk away from this horrible encounter.

"You are a strong one, able to have resisted a breaking, but this place is not for you, Francis Richard Briefer," she said with steady, clear voice. "I know that you occupied it in life, but that life is long gone now. You must move on."

The ghost-globe flared up then, suffusing the room with its sickly illumination. Though I would have wished for better circumstances to allow me to see once again, I was thankful for any clarity at the time. My lady stared at the ball of light before her, still speaking.

"Yes, there are things here that cause you pain and misery. The scores of people that come and go and ignore you, the lack of a stage…the absence of applause.

"And then the motion pictures. The men and women who seem to you to be actors, but who do not perform for an audience but for a select few. And the strange devices that capture their images but are in fact cold, lifeless things. This is not what you called the acting craft. This is not the *life* of the stage. This is not your world."

The sickly light grew dimmer at that. I steeled myself, unsure of what might come next. Dread gripped me again and the feeling that I should rabbit away from the scene before me. It was all I could do to maintain my position.

The light then advanced on my lady.

Her hand whipped into the pocket of her trousers, but came out empty. She looked down at her fingers as they opened and closed on nothing.

The ghost-globe drew past her and toward me.

Lady Janus swiveled on her heels and like a banshee out of hell screeched out loud and hurled herself after the light.

She dove around the ball of green light and, picking up a chair, swung it at the motion picture camera arrangement.

The chair crashed into the camera and its tripod stand, smashing it to the floor. When it impacted there, it broke into pieces.

The light globe halted, hung there in place.

"There!" bellowed my sweet lady. "There! I have conquered your demon! You owe me recompense!"

She jumped over to the pieces of the shattered camera and kicked them across the room. Then, turning back to the spirit of Francis Richard Briefer she fixed it with a look of unbridled rage.

"Now go!" she screamed at it. "I will not tell you again! Go! *Go!*"

The unearthly thing wavered in the air, as if unsure of itself. Finally, it retreated. As if mounting invisible stairs, it ascended toward the ceiling and in the space of merely a few heartbeats it was gone.

Light, natural light, returned to the room.

My lady stood there, still racked with fury, wild-eyed and heaving with dry sobs. I stared at her, not knowing what to do.

"Mr. Pettigrew said the man had vanished from the film."

"I'm not a bit surprised," she replied.

The road back to Mount Airy was open and free, devoid of other motorists. I took some pleasure from the feel of the automobile around me and the wind whipping through my hair. It seemed to clear out some of the cobwebs that had taken root in my head.

"Were the damages that extensive to the restaurant?" she asked after another bout of silence.

I glanced over at her, sitting on the seat beside me with her long black hair pushed back from her face by the wind. I admired her features for a moment and then answered.

"Don't know. Didn't really ask. Pettigrew seemed grateful enough to you and I didn't want to push the issue. I suppose he'll go over all that with Valerie Havelock-Mayer. We needn't worry about it, I suppose."

"We're fortunate that a fire didn't break out," she opined as I pulled up into the drive of Janus House and pointed the car at the garage.

"Yes," I agreed.

Parking the car, I set the brake and got out to come around and open her door. She took my proffered hand and alighted from the vehicle. We walked out of the garage and toward the front door of the house…her house.

"Joshua, something is missing."

I asked her what that might be, knowing that she referred to the two times I'd witnessed her reaching for something that simply wasn't there. She seemed awfully vexed by it all, but had no answer for it.

At the big front door of the mansion, my lady turned to me and, with an absence of emotion, mumbled a few words.

"Beg pardon, Lady Janus?"

Those alien eyes flashed and I racked up another point in my column.

"Why are you here?" she inquired.

"Why, every great hero needs a chronicler," I said.

"Quite," she responded, sans smile.

She moved toward the door. "Will you stay?" she asked over her shoulder, her eyes hidden from me.

I was taken a bit aback by that, though my heart jumped at it.

"It would be…improper for us to stay in this house together, alone," I said, lifting my chin.

She spun around to once again pierce me with her eyes. I could swear then that a slight smile played around her lips.

"Oh," she said, glancing at the great house, "we won't be alone…"

From:
Herbert Marshman Pettigrew
Owner, Reale Pictures Inc.

To:
All Departments

It is with great happiness and satisfaction that I am able to announce that we will be re-opening production on A WOMAN IN THE CITY. All departments are to return to work immediately. Please see your supervisors for assignments and our restructured timetable.

We have successfully concluded our dealings with the restaurant and settled on the damages to be paid to the establishment. We regret the unfortunate circumstances that led to this situation, but they were wholly unforeseen by myself and the company's officers. I wish I could offer a rational explanation as to what was witnessed on that strange and inexplicable day, but I find myself falling woefully short on that score.

Regardless, Reale Pictures is poised to move forward into a bright future and to put the entire debacle behind us. If anyone in any department is approached by or receives any communication of any sort from the two persons involved in the disruption of filming at the restaurant, please inform myself or Mr. Gayme without delay.

I would also like to express our regret at the loss of Mr. Ashton Clark as Director on A WOMAN IN THE CITY. We have heard that the sanitarium to which he was recently admitted is a pleasant place and we hope that it will serve to soothe his troubled mind and that he will return to us for future productions. We will be announcing his replacement shortly.

Also, I require the Print Department to please forward all existing, developed footage from A WOMAN IN THE CITY to my office, along with a projector.

Yours Truly,

H. M. Pettigrew
Chapter 3
Cutting the Strings

Chapter III
CUTTING THE STRINGS

Too often we become so immersed in our situation that we begin to ignore what is truly important, what is staring us right in the face. We make connections, tie things up with strings, and we believe ourselves to be invincible. We ignore the counsel of others because we believe that what we do, what we are interpreting from external stimuli, is the best course. And then mistakes are made.

This is the story of mistakes. *My* mistakes.

I began to explore Janus House shortly after taking up residence there. I guess that I fancied that I would conquer the manse, in a way, by walking its halls and opening its doors and divining its paths. I had no true idea of what was in store for me, an ant crawling around in a very, very big warren.

Looking into the house's every nook and cranny was not so immediately strange, not at first; the strangeness began at breakfast the very first morning after I had entered the structure.

My lady's attitude was of sour disposition to begin with as she had begun to dwell on thoughts of Valerie Havelock-Mayer. It seems the wealthy woman's strong disposition towards the name of Janus had caused my companion undue stress; why she gave the restaurateur the time of day let alone continued thought was beyond me.

Still, my lady *was* bothered by it all and it was beginning to take a toll on her own usually-level manners. Then, the other shoe dropped.

"You may enter any room you like in this house, save one," she said to me over a steaming cup of rather good coffee. Those were her exact words.

Had I suddenly found myself in a Bartok opera? Did my lady think me ignorant of basic folktales? Yes, my hackles rose; just a bit. Then the humor of the scene presented itself. I chuckled. Anger flashed in her eyes.

"And what room would that be, Lady Janus?" I asked, risking it all.

She described the area of the house and the door in question. Feeling bold, I inquired then as to why this must be that I should not enter the room? I assumed then that she was having me on, that below her seeming ire my lady was testing my sense of the absurd or perhaps the limits of my propriety. After all, I was a guest at Janus House, and she its presumed mistress.

"There is no key," she answered plainly enough. "I do not wish you to force the lock. Please respect my wishes."

I nodded, not wanting to force the *issue*. She got up from the table and stalked off, heading toward whatever it was that she did to pass her days. I sighed and removed myself. If there were servants to clear away the breakfast dishes, I'd leave them to it though to this day I have never seen another soul in the house besides myself and my lady.

Living soul, that is.

Janus House; how shall I describe it in mere words?

A warren, a maze, a labyrinth. I half expected to run across a Minotaur on my sojourns through its many passages, halls, rooms and, yes, doors.

There is no other place like it on Earth, of that I'm sure. For the sheer complexity of its architectural anomalies it deserves to be memorialized, if for nothing else. It is also deceptive; when one turns a corner in Janus House, all bets are off. What you believe lies ahead of you is rarely what you expect. And why one would have any expectations at all after spending no more than ten minutes in the old mansion is something I can't fathom.

One of the most astounding things I discovered is not only the enormous duplication of rooms, but also the sheer wastefulness of space. As a professional layabout, I had come to possess a keen eye for rooms; one does not cool one's heels for extended stretches of time without becoming overly familiar with one's surroundings. But Janus House baffled me. There was little to no rhyme or reason in its composition.

In my first day of exploration, I counted eight different sitting rooms. On the second day, six more. While in my third day I racked up an amazing tally of thirteen different sitting rooms. On the fourth day I came across no sitting rooms at all, but discovered three kitchens, two dining rooms, a ballroom, and an area I guessed to be a sauna of sorts. Fifth day brought more sitting rooms, three in all. On the sixth day I encountered a most beautiful room filled with aquariums of various sizes.

On the seventh day, I rested. And where I rested was, to that moment, my most favorite room of all.

Before I continue, I must make a quick not here about the *sounds* that fill Janus House. All manner of sounds, from what seemed to be singing off in the distance to the clanking of pots and pans and even a train whistle, though there are no train tracks nearby; none that I have found, to be clear about it. In all, the house produces sounds like we living beings breath. There are always sounds within its walls.

Save for the room in which I came to rest. It was a library, you see. And that makes all the difference in the world.

As you may already guess, the room was filled with books. Shelves and shelves and shelves of books, and in-between the books there were displays of objects. Many of these objects were of antique vintage and after a few moments of looking over them, I realized a theme that ran through many of them: militariana.

The books? Oh, they had themes that encompassed the wide world, perhaps even the universe. History, science, geography; all well represented. In addition, I viewed a staggering number of volumes on what I would call more esoteric subjects; the occult, the extra-normal, that sort of stuff.

It all clicked then. My lady's knowledge of these matters. Her odd behavior. Oh, I didn't yet have a clear line of deduction for it, no way to lay it out in words, but inside, it made sense on a sympathetic level. This was her *home*. She belonged here, despite the overwhelming *maleness* of the place.

I plunked myself down in a large, comfortable chair of deep red velvet and picked at random a tome to peruse. It was then I discovered the absence of sounds in the library save for a ticking clock and, for a fleeting moment, I was happy.

After an hour or so in pleasurable pursuit of a rare species of butterfly found in *The Seduction of the Amazon* a strong sense of unease began to creep into my day. This flowed into melancholy and that into depression.

I could not stop thinking about the room I was forbidden to enter. I had become one of Bluebeard's brides, much to my chagrin.

Before I knew what was happening, I found myself in the corridor that led to the room in question. Damn me, but perhaps my lady knew me better and more thoroughly than I had imagined. Perhaps she knew me better than I knew myself. My feeling of unease increased at the thought.

Up until that moment, my interaction with Lady Janus had been something of a game for me, the filling of a hole in my existence. I had nothing better to do, so why not chase off after a mysterious woman who herself chased after ghosts? It seemed logical at the time, but once I was immersed in the proceedings I could not shake the feeling that I had gotten myself mired in something much more than merely a game.

Down the corridor I spotted the door to the room. It seemed much like any other door in the manse; if I had passed by it unknowing of its queer pedigree, I'd have gone on unknowing. It did not stand out from the rest.

The lure of it was a powerful thing. The pull on me it exhibited shocked me, as if it were a living creature drawing me in by way of an ancient snare. I fought it. Beside me, in the corridor, I spied another door out of the corner of my eye. I had not seen it before, so focused was I on my true goal.

To avoid one door, I entered another.

I stepped swiftly through the portal and shut the door behind me, perhaps a bit too noisily. I waited a beat, then one more, and turned to view my new surroundings.

I had entered a room that, had my mood been more cheerful, I might have called charming. It was decorated tastefully, with a fine balance between the male and female sensibilities and with a small, crackling fire in its fireplace. There was one window, but its shades and curtains were drawn tightly shut and, interestingly, the only furniture present were two chairs, both of them comfortable-looking and facing each other in roughly the center of the room.

Suddenly tired, I took to one of the chairs. Though I had not intended to nap, something akin to sleep overtook me and I visited a very rough patch of what could laughingly be called slumber. After an indefinable passage of time, I awoke with a start to the sound of a door opening and closing.

Strangely, the sound did not come from behind me, from the direction of the door through which I had entered the room.

I opened my eyes to the sight of a girl.

The temperature in the room had fallen dramatically, despite the little fire in the hearth. I could actually see my breath. I did not discern the girl's.

She was a sweet thing, dressed in a simple gown of cream and with only the barest of decoration to it. I presumed her to be around twenty years of age, give or take a year, with a face that, while mature with its pale blue eyes and dusky red lips, still encompassed a small amount of baby fat. Overall, she was very pale, with a snowy complexion, platinum hair worn long, and a good figure. The girl's movements were smooth and sure as she stepped around the room, lighting from one spot to another. It reminded me of a butterfly.

I had spent little time in Lady Janus' world but my mind leapt to a conclusion and I guessed then that I might be viewing a spirit.

Boldly, or so I thought, I attempted to speak to the girl. This had no effect on her, for she continued walking around, examining the room and its trappings. She did not come near me, though, but whether or not that was due to my presence, I could not tell at the moment. I spoke up again and then a third time, but still no reaction. Some spirit investigator I was turning out to be; my first solo encounter with the Unknown and I was muffing it up quite thoroughly.

Suddenly, and without any provocation, she turned to look at me.

I should like to say that I awoke some time later in the library but that would be an untruth. That I found myself once again among that splendid collection of books and ephemera is true enough, but that I arrived there through the vehicle of sleep is fudging it a bit. I do not know exactly how I came to be in the library after my visitation with the girl; I was looking at her looking at me and then I was fondling the spine of a very old tome on the architecture of London's waterfront district.

Of course I assumed I had fallen asleep in the library and dreamed the entire encounter. Anybody in my position would assume the same. But I felt that to be inaccurate and I decided then and there that I would revisit the quaint little sitting room the next day and prove to myself that it was more of reality than of the dream landscape.

You see, the girl's slight smile as she swung her attention to me haunted my inner vision.

The next morning over breakfast I spoke of several innocuous things to my dark lady, she was focused on an article in the daily *Mount Airy Eagle* concerning Valerie Havelock-Mayer, but kept mum on my ghostly encounter of the previous day. Instead, I talked of books.

"I'm not sure I care for you to be traipsing through the library," said she, finally raising her head from the newspaper.

I frowned at her. "Beg pardon, but I thought it was only one single room I was not to enter?"

She matched my frown. "Yes," she admitted after a silent moment, "that is what I asked of you. Do as you will, Joshua, but please harm nothing."

Wiping my mouth of crumbs and taking a last swig of coffee, I bid her good day and left my lady to the remains of her breakfast. Minutes later I hated myself for the exchange, but what was done was done; the air between us could be cleared later.

I returned then to what I began to think of as the Room of Visitation.

Having settled myself into the chair facing away from the door, I closed my eyes and pictured the girl. It occurred to me that this would be the proper way to, in essence, "call" to her.

I sat like that for close to an hour, as I reckoned it, until finally I once again heard the sound of a door opening and then closing. I opened my eyes to find the girl sitting in the chair across from me, gazing upon me with that same slight smile as before.

I bit down on my tongue. This was new territory for me, despite the well and the restaurant experiences. I felt then that I could be making a mistake by speaking to her…it…whatever the apparition before me might be.

She said nothing. No sound issued from her, not even when she had sat down nor made a small adjustment to her gown; the vision was absolutely silent. I began to think that. Indeed, it *was* nothing more than that. A vision. An image from the past. A photograph from an earlier time that moved.

The girl may not even have been looking at me, but perhaps someone else, long gone.

She was very pretty; my initial appraisal of the day before was accurate. I also saw in her a thread of melancholy, not unlike my own, but I tamped down any further feeling that we may have been kindred spirits in that. It was not danger that I sensed, per se, but more a wariness of too much empathy towards an unliving thing. For you see, it could have been nothing more, nothing less than just that.

This is what the reasonable, logical part of my brain told me. The foolish, lonely part loosened my tongue and opened my mouth.

I began to tell the girl of myself.

Later, I slipped from the room and back down the corridor to my own quarters. The day had passed and night was falling. I hurried to spruce myself up for dinner, trying hard not to act the part of a wayward spouse covering for a lapse in judgment with another woman.

A third visitation occurred. I talked and my young lady listened? I wasn't quite sure if that were the case, but the fantasy remained intact for through the fourth and fifth visitation.

On the sixth day of visiting the room, I paused in my rambling and leaned forward in my chair. I had never made such a motion before then. I suddenly wanted to see what the girl might do, how she might react.

As I bent forward, my eyes never leaving hers, I felt a hand on my shoulder.

"Joshua, no."

My dark lady. Found me out. Stopped me in my tracks.

I jumped up and wheeled around to face her, red-faced and ashamed. She narrowed her unnerving eyes at me; I wondered how like a madman I must have looked.

"Yes, *Lady Janus?*" I threw at her. "How may I be of service?"

"Please, Joshua; come with me," she beckoned, taking my hand.

Surprised at my words, I told her that I could not do so for I was very obviously otherwise engaged. I motioned over my shoulder with my chin to emphasize my point.

My lady appeared very serious. She peered over my shoulder, shook her head slightly.

"See for yourself, my friend."

I needn't look. I knew for a certainty that we were quite alone in the room.

Outside in the corridor, after shutting the door to the Room of Visitation, my emotions got the better of me. I hastily informed the mistress of the house that I would gather my things and leave.

"Joshua, listen to me," she said calmly. "I have known all along that you have been visiting that room." My hackles rose; I tried to protest, but she cut me off.

"I know most everything that occurs in this house." Her eyes left mine looked aside. "Somehow it's most strange. But, regardless, I care very much for your safety. Perhaps it was foolish of me to bring you into the house, but I'm not thinking very clearly of late. It seemed a good thing to do at the time; you seem a strong young man and open-minded. But now…"

"You gave me only one stipulation to my staying here," I reminded her, "and I have completely adhered to that." It was not the full truth, of course, for I had lusted after the forbidden room in my heart, but I was not about to tell my lady that. "If there are more such stipulations, *you need only tell me*."

The dark woman twisted her shoulders and swiveled her head around. Her lovely black tresses moved with her and I heard the bones in her neck pop. She turned and stepped over to the wall of the corridor opposite me.

"My dear Joshua, I barely know you. I barely know myself. How can I tell you anything other than what I know at this time?" Amazingly, she laid her forehead against the wallpaper, as if its surface my cool her fevered thoughts.

I could see a weight upon her. It sat heavily over her entire carriage. I wondered at that, why it must be so.

I assumed that weight's label to read "Roman Janus."

"Is this your mansion" I asked her.

She did not turn from her examination of the far wall. "I…I believe so. Yes. It must be."

My lady then spun around to look at me.

"And yet, I have memories of another place, a far simpler home than this one, and people there who cared for me and loved me. But I left them, for some reason. I did not want to, but something forced me to leave.

"Joshua, that does not matter now. You are in distress yourself, and I want to help you. Does…does the spirit in that room somehow touch your heart?"

I nodded without hesitation. "Then," she continued, "…let me – *us* try to help *it*."

We returned to the room and shut the door behind us.

"I call it the Room of Visitation," I informed my companion. She looked all around it and then at me.

"The room told you that. Perhaps you are settling in more than either of us had imagined."

My lady motioned for me to take the chair once again. I did so and then felt both her hands on my shoulders as she took a spot behind me. Her touch was, like her eyes, unnerving and yet also a source of confidence for me: the mistress of Janus House would be able to conquer any question the structure could throw at us.

"Call her to you," Lady Janus said. "Summon the spirit. You need not be afraid; I am with you."

I resisted the urge to correct her. Maybe it wasn't the most solid of foundations for a launch into the spirit world, but I wanted no more strife between us. I closed my eyes and thought of the girl.

Several minutes passed. The familiar sound of the opening door came to my ears.

"She is here," said my lady.

I looked to see the young girl standing behind the other chair, not sitting in it. Her position and stance reflected that of my companion and I pondered the implications of that. Was there to be strife there, too?

"What do you want, spirit?" asked my lady. "Why do you appear in this room?"

The girl's eternal silence was in full force. I searched her pale countenance for some sign of the smile she most always had for me, but found it wholly absent. I opened my mouth to speak, but my lady tightened her grip on my shoulders slightly and continued to address the spirit.

"Can you tell us who you are? Are you troubled?"

Nothing. No recognition at all.

"You must tell us *something* if we are to help you," said my companion. I could hear a sliver of stress insert itself into her words. I did not like what I foresaw in the coming moments.

"She has never spoken before, not to me at least," said I. "But she has listened…or at least I believe she has listened."

"Joshua, quiet," whispered Lady Janus, somewhat sternly.

The girl's eyes narrowed, nostrils flared.

"We must end this," my lady said. My hackles rose yet again and I surged to offer argument. Strong hands, like that of a *man*, forced me back down again.

"Spirit, begone! Break your ties to this plane!

"*Go thee to thy rest, oh shade! Thou hast served well in life, now take thy reward!*"

There they were: the words I did not want to hear, the words I did not want my companion to speak. But, there they were.

The genie had been let out of the bottle.

Lady Janus and I discovered ourselves to be no longer in the Room of Visitation but once more outside in the corridor in the wink of an eye.

She reached for the doorknob, clearly angry.

I reached out, caught her wrist and pulled it away.

"No."

She centered on me, her anger flashing about her eyes like a miniature thunderstorm.

"Release me, Joshua. You don't know what you're saying. That *spirit* must be broken! It's my business to see to the welfare of this house and that *thing* in there cannot stand! It's detrimental to everything around us, can't you *see* that? Are you so blinded by it?"

She was raving, or so I thought at that moment. I asked myself for the hundredth time what I had gotten myself into. She, the house, ghosts…I was out of my depth.

But I knew, somehow *knew* that the girl in the room wouldn't harm me or anyone else for that matter. Yes, I felt then that I knew better than my lady on the subject.

I took both her hands in mine, tightly, and asked her…*implored* her to trust *me* as I had trusted her before. I asked her to leave well enough alone and to allow me to cut my ties with the girl on my own terms. No one else's. Mine and mine alone.

I promised my lady that everything would be all right.

But what did I know?

My companion walked off after a bit, looking tired and drawn. I watched her back as she went, then slipped back into the Room of Visitation. The guilt of it all hung heavily around my neck, like the legendary albatross.

Interestingly, the girl was there as I entered, as if she were waiting for me.

I took my usual chair and settled into it, though my nerves were raw and frayed. For several minutes I could not meet the spirit's gaze, but finally, I raised my eyes to her and, in a flood of words, poured out my soul to her.

I tried to explain my companion's situation, or at least as much as I knew of it then, but the words began to sound hollow, like excuses a child creates to justify a fib or the snatching of a piece of candy. I had no real right to speak of my lady to the girl, but I found my tongue to be loose and speech dripping from it. I grew hot with shame but I did not pause in my soul-cleansing.

When I had finished, I saw that the girl's expression had not changed throughout my talk. It remained beatific? Patient? Or perhaps disinterested?

I got up to leave, sure at that time that I never wanted to return to that room.

The girl held up a hand. I stopped.

It was the greatest interaction that we had yet.

With silent calm, she rose from her chair and I descended back into mine. The girl turned away from me and began a slow circuit around the room. We had seemingly returned to square one. This was how we had begun.

Finally, she came to rest near a small table, one that I had seen before but took no real notice of. She reached out with one hand and placed something on the table. I blinked; I had not previously observed anything in her hand, but she most definitely had set an object on the table.

I rose from my chair. Did I dare approach the table, approach *her*? Feeling as if I had little to lose, I stepped around the chairs and took a hesitant step in her direction. She did not move. Erring on the side of caution, I approached the small table from the opposite direction, so as to not...what? Frighten her away?

Regardless, I stopped with the table between us. It was the closest I had come to the girl.

She smiled at me. Not the slight smile of before, but a real smile. Confused, I could only stare at her face, thinking how lovely it was.

Her eyes dipped downward, to the table's top, then back up to meet mine. I took her hint, finally, and looked down at the table myself.

There, on its lacquered surface, rested a small, dark disk.

At first glance, I took it to be a pure circle, perhaps of metal or even stone, but on examination I could see that the object was more like a geometric shape, with multiple flat edges, some exceedingly minute. I cannot say that the disk appeared old, for every time I tried to mentally gauge its age, it seemed to change. It may have been ancient, but it also may have been made only a year before.

I reached out to pick it up, half-expecting the girl to stop me. She did not. Holding it, the disk felt cool and smooth on my fingers, but not like a dead thing; more like a piece of machinery that had recently been pulled from a greater mechanism and cooled down with water.

My inclination was to then turn it over and view the side of it that faced the table.

A snap of static electricity bit into my right ear and caused the hair there to stand on end. I looked up at the girl.

She shook her head from side to side: a clear indication that I was not to proceed with my inclination.

So be it. I bowed to the girl, unsure of what had just transpired or what I had been gifted with. Deep down inside, though, I sensed it was all connected somehow to my dark lady.

Maybe, just maybe, this was what was missing from Lady Janus' troubled life.

I stepped from the room into a tempest.

A storm had whipped up outside Janus House, though inside the Room of Visitation it had been calm and serene. In the hallway, the deluge pounded upon the roof of the old mansion and lightning snapped and hissed in snatches seen through windows. The very air sizzled with its periodic bursts. Strange shadows waved back and forth across the wallpaper.

One such shadow, at the far end of the corridor, caught my eye.

A snap of lightning illuminated the area, bringing the shadow into sharp relief. It appeared to be a man, standing there, unmoving. I squinted; unsure of what I was seeing, but again a burst of light clarified the phenomenon.

My sense of it was that of a male, a bit taller than myself and of straight spine and good bearing. Beyond that, there were no details I could discern, save for a niggling thought that it might be the shadow of a soldier.

Rationalization flooded into me and I assumed that a coat rack or even a tailor's dummy stood at the end of the hallway, just out of sight around a corner. I knew that if I would only step to the side, the entire thing would take on another perspective; a singularly earthly one.

I took a step to the right and looked again. There was nothing there to cast the shadow.

Silently, I asked for absolution from the scenario. I knew with a certainty what would come next and I did not care to see it. But, it came.

As the rain increased, the shadow of the man raised one arm and extended an index finger, pointing at something I assumed to be in close proximity to itself.

The door. *The* door.

I found myself gripping the disk in my hand so forcefully that its odd edges bit into the flesh. I shook with...rage? With fear? I'm certain of so much, but at that moment I could not begin to describe the emotions coursing through me. For a life-long layabout, I had been thrown into one situation after another that forced me into mental work of a kind I did not care much for. If only I would be granted a respite!

Why was the thing pointing at that door? I was forbidden to enter that room! But by whom? A madwoman, perhaps, or, at the very least, an amnesiac with delusions of another life.

I was going mad myself, certainly. What else could explain the things I had seen? The things I'd experienced? Were they some sort of mass-hysteria grafted by my lady onto me? Or...good Lord... were they all part of some elaborate ruse?

It was a line of thought and deduction that ill-suited me. I was in a house, however fantastic, and could hear the rain on its very solid roof. I held a physical object in my hand given to me by a ghost, yes, yes! But that was neither here nor there! I was still in possession of all my faculties, such as they were, I was sure of it. I would continue to take on the world one oddity at a time.

An immense, sonorous clap of thunder went off just then, shaking the very timbers of the house and setting my ears to ringing. Stars danced before my eyes and when they had cleared, the shadow at the end of the corridor had disappeared.

The reverberations of the thunder lasted for long seconds, sending a vase on a small table in the middle of the hallway crashing to the floor. I jumped as it smashed into bits.

I stood there in the semi-darkness, listening to the passing storm, wondering where I might find my lady in the house.

"Joshua?"

Somehow, I remained in my skin, but not by much. Lady Janus had found me, apparently.

She'd come up from behind me, carrying a candle in one hand and her skirts in another. Feeling unexpectedly chivalrous, I resisted an urge to take the candle from her and comfort her. It was an odd thought, for my lady very rarely looks the part of a maiden in distress.

"The electricity's gone out," she informed me. I stared at her in wonder, for I had not noticed that it was gone. I continued to stare at her, choosing my next words and actions carefully. After a long moment, my dark lady actually smiled and cast her eyes downward, almost demurely.

"Joshua, why do you look at me like that?"

"Hold out your hand," I told her, affixing a serious expression upon my face.

Her queerly-set eyes narrowed; her smile very nearly disappearing. There was a minute shake of her head.

Now I smiled. "What? You think I've got a nice toad or asp to give you?"

That made some sort of impression on her, very clearly. She raised her hand to her mouth, covering it almost completely. Her eyes were wide and...innocent? Before my gaze, my lady seemed to transform into someone else. Someone younger, less knowing of the world, less experienced.

"Why," she whispered, "why would that mean something to me?"

"A beau?" I offered. "Or a rake who once gifted you with some squirmy, squishy denizen of a pond, or a...a..." I paused, frustrated that the moment was passing and becoming something entirely else.

"Dammit, hold out your hand..."

She did, though slowly, warily. In her open palm, I placed the disk, with its face downward.

My lady said nothing at first, simply looked at the object in her hand. Seconds ticked by, then perhaps a full minute. Still she remained silent. The air between us felt frigid.

"This," she said, finally, "is *his*."

There were many things I guessed she might have said or even done, but that wasn't exactly one of them. I *knew* who she meant, of course, but the pieces of the puzzle remained jumbled and vexing.

I ventured a question. "Is *this* what you've been looking for? What has been missing?"

"*Where* did you get this?" she asked, her face cast down, her eyes completely hidden from me. The scent of lavender came to my nose, pungent and strong.

Well, that *was* a question, wasn't it? I began to stammer out a reply, feeling my way through its morass.

My lady would have none of it. She flipped her face upwards and I saw there a stranger, livid and possessed of a singular fury.

"She had no *business* giving this to *you!*"

Lady Janus' eyes rolled up in their sockets, leaving almost nothing but white. I reeled back, horrified. Then, she began to look over my shoulder. At the Room of Visitation. I grew very anxious, very swiftly.

"No," I said, as plainly and as full of command as I could muster.

"Joshua, please! Step out of the way!"

"No."

Her countenance looked all together like a man's then, stern and building up a good head of steam. I was fearful under its baleful presence. Under no circumstances could I allow her to enter that room.

My lady flung herself at me. I caught her wrists, but, in doing so, I let go of the candle. It tumbled to the floor and was soon forgotten in the struggle. She gritted her teeth and tried to wrest herself from my grasp, even resorting to kicking my shins with her manly boots, but I held on and attempted to drive her back, away from the door she had made her target.

"Stop!" I bellowed. "Lady Janus, please stop! You aren't in your right mind!"

As if I had thrown a bucket of cold water over her, she shrank away from me, her mouth moving but no words coming from it. After a moment, she seemed to collect herself and looked up at me. Her face looked normal or as normal as it had ever looked.

"Joshua," she said with a twist to her mouth. "Joshua, I believe I am all right now. Look, here; I shall put the disk away." She dropped the object into a pocket of her skirt, hiding it completely.

"Now, we need to discuss what we will do about the spirit in that room."

Some of the old Lady Janus had come rushing back into her; I could hear it in her voice and in her carriage. She crossed her arms and rubbed at her chin with one hand. Then leaning back against the wall behind her, she appeared to be in deep thought.

I stepped over to her. "Well, why does anything *have* to be done about her...it?"

Something suddenly flew into my line of sight and it was as if some vaudevillian had dropped one of those impossibly large weights on my head. Again, I saw stars.

Lady Janus rushed past me, dropping the small statue of a goat she acquired from a table behind her back and with which she had beaned me.

"I'm sorry, my dear boy," I heard her say, "but it is imperative that I rid this world of such spirits."

Dazed, I tried to pick myself up off the floor, but could not find my feet. A salty trickle of wetness down the side of my face and to the corner of my mouth told me my injuries were not going to win me any awards for comeliness. Then I heard a door open.

I scrambled around and crawled towards the room. When I reached the doorframe, I attempted to rise by using it to pull myself up but succeeded only in bringing a new wave of dizziness and nausea down around me. Looking up, I saw my lady walking into the center of the room. I implored her to stop, feebly, but she ignored me.

"Spirit!" she called out. "Spirit, heed me and appear! I am the master of this house and you are not welcome here! I command you to *appear!*"

There was no sound of opening and closing doors that time. The ghost of the girl simply was there.

I held back the vomit crawling its way up from me, knowing the inevitable outcome of the play that unspooled before me. I could no more stop it then I could stop the storm that still crashed overhead.

"Will you leave under your own power?" asked Lady Janus of the spirit. The girl looked calm, unruffled by the...the...*spirit-breaker* that confronted her. "Or will you force me to sever the strings that hold you to this mortal sphere?"

The girl's face remained passive, unchanged. I could not see my lady's face, but I guessed it to be severe.

Then, the ghost spread her arms out from her sides, with her palms facing my lady, composed and collected. I saw a small hardness also come into her expression as she locked her gaze upon she who proclaimed herself the master of Janus House.

Perhaps my lady took the gesture as a sign of readiness to do battle; of this I am not sure. Regardless, she acted and acted swiftly.

The disk was suddenly in her hand and its face was exposed to the girl.

The girl screamed.

It was something on the side of the disk that I could not see that caused the spirit to contort in silent expressions of intense pain. Her image wavered, like smoke from a fire fanned by the wind, and then it broke up into small wisps of steam. And then it was gone.

A great rushing came into the room, a hurricane blast that tore at my lady and sent me tumbling backwards over the threshold and out into the corridor. I whipped my head around to see the door to the room slam shut with a loud crash, utterly cutting me off from my companion.

Finally able to gain my feet again, I flung myself upon the wooden panels of the door and beat upon it with both fists, shouting for my lady, but to no avail; the portal remained closed and locked.

I must have hit my head again after I fell to the floor when I found that no efforts of mine could re-open the door. The winds had been cut off from the closing of it, and the hallway was very still and quiet. I lay there for a long time, and then lapsed into slumber, my face wet and hot from my tears.

A jolt of prickly pain woke me some time later. I opened my eyes to look into a pair of crystals, metallic-looking and cold. Within them floated tiny flecks of iron shavings, small triangles that spun and cavorted of their own accord.

I pulled back to take in the face that framed the twin crystals and found some warmth there. The nose on the face was strong and the lips below it full and inviting – if it were an angel, I would have to compliment our Creator on His eye for detail in his helpers.

"Joshua, does it hurt?" asked my lady.

"Very much so," I replied, wincing. "If you were to continue to press on it, I'm quite sure I will pass out again. If you feel no need for my company, then have at it."

"Joshua, the room is empty."

I pondered that. "Then she…the spirit…?"

Lady Janus sat back and folded her legs up in front of her, sitting on the floor by my side like a Red Indian. "Yes, gone, and the room, also. Completely empty. A shell, nothing more."

I sighed then, letting a bit more of my feelings show than I had intended. The die had been cast and mistakes made. There was an entire list of them now, so many to consider and precious few to be corrected.

Do you remember what I wrote earlier? "Too often we become so immersed in our situation that we begin to ignore what is truly important, what is staring us right in the face. We make connections, tie things up with strings, and we believe ourselves to be invincible. We ignore the counsel of others because we believe that what we do, what we are interpreting from external stimuli, is the best course. And then mistakes are made."

I had become smitten with someone who listened to me, truly *listened* to me, and I had tied myself to her. Then, I couldn't see what was right below my nose: danger, I presume, and more.

I had it on good authority. The Spirit-Breaker had returned, you see.

I looked over at my lady and searched her face for some hint of that which I had originally seen in her, there at that little café in Canal Chichester, but precious little of it was evident at that moment. She had found her calling, really found it, and I could see that if she was not devoted to it before, our further adventures, if there were to be any, would prove that dedication.

"What is on that disk?" I asked.

"I don't know," she answered. "Perhaps nothing. Nothing at all.'"

I asked her why she sounded as if she was quoting someone, but she had no reply for that.

"I do know that no one may look at its face, no one alive, that is. I once saw someone look at it."

I sat up quickly, bringing myself further misery from my split head. "And...?"

My lady clenched the disk tightly.

"And it drove them quite insane."

I spent the next few days in bed in my room, recovering from the blow to my noggin. My lady cleaned it and stitched it and dressed it, and I marveled at her proficiency in doing so. She had very definite medical skills, but I couldn't drag anything about them out of her.

When I felt better, I began to take walks through the hallways and corridors of Janus House, testing my abilities and growing stronger all the while.

I had hoped for a happy ending to this particular tale, but I'm afraid I do not have one to offer. In fact, something occurred on one of those strolls of mine that weakened my resolve for the whole affair even while my body grew strong.

I had come upon the door to the Room of Visitation one evening and, after some reflection, opened it and stepped inside. I found the room to be just as Lady Janus described it.

Empty. A barren shell. Even the wallpaper was gone.

Turning to leave, I thought I heard noises out in the hallway and, not wanting to bring a frown to my lady's face over my folly and curiosity; I very gingerly opened the door and peered out into the darkened corridor.

There, at its far end, I saw the door to the room there open. That room.

Lady Janus exited the room and then shut the door behind her.

She had lied to me.

Prominent Lawyer Passes

Jasper Forthing, a prominent Mount Airy lawyer, has died at the age of seventy-three. On the evening of August 4, Mr. Farthing suffered a heart attack in his home at No. 22 Bentley Blvd., and was pronounced dead some minutes later. He is survived by his wife Gentian; his four children, Abigail, Louella, Primrose, and Jinkster; and eighteen assorted grandchildren.

Mr. Forthing began his career as a solicitor after returning from abroad at the age of twenty-two and quickly rose to prominence among regional peers. He joined the firm of Farley, Winkle, Munger & Munger as a junior partner at age thirty-one and made a full partner only three years later. The firm of Farley, Farthing, Munger & Munger went on to establish itself as the preeminent source for legal representation in the district, due in large part to Mr. Forthing's attention to detail and a steadfast drive to succeed, according to his partners.

Mr. Forthing worked for many years as the attorney of Valerie Havelock-Mayer, owner and proprietress of La Maison d'Havelock in the city, and was instrumental in the protracted settlements that stemmed from the late Richard Mayer's will and testament.

The late solicitor will be interred at Whispering Oaks Cemetery after a brief showing at Gateman Mortuary. Both services will be open only to the immediate family and invited friends and associates.

An unusual codicil to Mr. Forthing's last will and testament states that should he "return to the mortal plane in any shape or form after legal and binding death, be it shade, revenant, ghoul or ghast," the solicitor resolutely bans "the presence of one Sgt. Roman Janus from the Forthing properties and holdings, ad infinitum." The addendum further states that, should Mr. Forthing's supposed spirit appear at any place other than his own properties or holdings, he asks the Mount Airy government and police department for their "kind indulgence to restrain the aforementioned person, or any representative of that person, from acting in any manner or fashion whatsoever detrimental to the shade, revenant, ghoul or ghast."

A reporter approached Mrs. Forthing for clarification of the unusual codicil, but was told by a family servant that the woman was deep in mourning and that her husband's wishes would be carried out to the letter of the law.

Sgt. Roman Janus could not be reached for comment.

From T*he Mount Airy Eagle*
Early Edition - Monday, August 6

Chapter IV
THE WHISPERING WALLPAPER
OF CHRISTMAS HALL

I remember – what do I remember? I remember how good the
wind felt whipping at my face and through my hair as we drove over
hill and dale and away from Janus House. Such a feeling of libera-
tion. Who knew then that our little vacation would serve to cloud
our minds even more?

My lady and I did not speak much to each other after the incident
of the Room of Visitation. For days following we seemed to avoid
confrontation, though I will admit that the avoidance was more on
my part than anything. I felt all-together betrayed after learning that
the very room that was barred to me was not so closed off to her.

Then an invitation came in the daily mail.

Seems there was some sort of annual gathering off in the countryside, somewhere on the outskirts of the great woods, at a place
with the charming name of Christmas Hall. My lady read the invitation with great interest and I saw a fire being stoked within her
as she did so. I resigned myself then and there to the certainty of a
journey that lay ahead of us.

I told myself it was a good thing, a chance to clear the air between
us, until I spied the envelope in which the invitation arrived. It was
addressed to Sgt. Roman Janus of Janus House.

My dark lady's compulsion to usurp the sergeant's belongings
knew no bounds, apparently, but instead of taking her to task over
such an abhorrent thing as opening another person's mail I kept
my counsel and smiled and nodded when she informed me that we
would be spending a weekend at Christmas Hall.

Over the next twenty-four hours as we prepared to depart on our sojourn into the great outdoors, I had a long talk with myself. Would it be so bad? I inquired, ruminating over the trip. Perhaps putting a distance of many miles between my companion and the strange house in which we played at domestic tranquility would be good for her suffering mind – and my own, for that matter.

I was feeling fairly cheerful about the situation when I brought the Lincoln around from the garage and to the front of the house, but the sight of Lady Janus alighting from its porch set a small dark squall over my head once more.

She was wearing trousers.

It was becoming quite a habit of mine, a bad habit, of saying nothing as the world crumbled around me, but I had made up my mind to keep our differences down to a low growl and only gave her one short look of distaste for her choice of apparel. If my lady noticed, she too remained mum.

We drove. On the outskirts of Mount Airy, I really opened her up and we chugged along into a seemingly gorgeous day.

It was, oh, perhaps twenty miles or so along our route when I noticed we were being followed.

I informed my lady. To her credit, she did not spin around in her seat to make out our followers but simply asked if I had my revolver. Well, it wasn't "my" revolver, but I patted my coat pocket in answer and gave the Lincoln a bit more gas.

Up ahead I saw the edges of the great woods, dark and foreboding. I knew our turn-off would be on our left and soon, but I did not decrease my speed. Feeling foolhardy, I gripped the wheel and told my companion to hang on tight.

The turn-off arrived on schedule and I jerked the wheel for a quick turn. We took it on two tires and I swear I heard something give below us, underneath the automobile. Somehow, it held together through the ungainly action.

Braking hard after the turn, I spun around in my seat and watched the main road for our pursuers. Seconds ticked by and no other motorcar was to be seen or heard. After a half-minute, I slammed our vehicle into gear and sped off down the little road of the turn-off.

"Well, *that* was fun, wasn't it?" I shouted to my lady. She furrowed her brow and remained silent.

Soon, Christmas Hall loomed large in our vision.

An immense old structure, it sat among the trees like a gigantic, aged bulldog. I had read up on the place before we left Janus House and learned that it was originally built some hundred and twenty years before as a home for a reclusive ship's captain who'd struck it rich in the Aleutians or someplace. Had the place constructed from the wood of his sailing vessel and then died within a few days of its completion. Changed hands over the years more than once, but had been transformed into a kind of resort for the well-to-do about thirty years ago.

Its current owner was a man named Lord Harry Christmas. No, I swear it.

I parked the Lincoln among a grouping of other automobiles and together my lady and I walked up the path to the hall. We were greeted at its front door by Lord and Lady Christmas themselves.

I suppose I expected a personage along the lines of Moore's poem or Nast's illustrations, but in reality, Harry Christmas was a tall, thin sort of chap with a full head of salt-and-pepper hair, great mutton chops of whiskers, warm hands and a faint scent of lemons about him. His wife could have been his sister, so similar where they in appearance; that is, sans facial hair.

His look of joy at another arriving guest melted into one of confusion when he apparently failed to recognize my companion and me.

"My invitation," said my lady, holding out the item in question to be taken from her. Christmas looked down at it, clearly befuddled. He and his wife then looked at each other and then back to my lady.

"Perhaps there's been some mistake," he said with a great rumbling voice. "This invitation was sent to our friend Sgt. Janus." He searched my lady's face an answer to the alleged mix-up.

"I don't believe there has been any mistake," replied my companion, "for it plainly arrived at my home. And here we are."

I thought quickly, and spoke up, hoping to avoid an ugly and unpleasant embarrassment for all involved parties.

"My, uh, lord and lady, my name is Joshua Hargreaves and I speak for, ah, *Lady* Janus here when I say that the, umm, sergeant is indisposed at this time and…sent us along in his stead. Are we welcome?"

It was exceedingly lame, I know, but our would-be hosts took it in stride after a moment's hesitation and Lord Christmas himself proclaimed that "any sister of Roman's" was a sister of *his* and that the beautiful lady and her handsome young friend – no embroidery of my own there, I promise – were of course welcome to Christmas Hall and to please enter in good spirits.

Sensing my lady's irritation over our host's presumption of her standing and nearly choking on the word *spirits*, I thanked the Christmases and we stepped over the threshold into our latest adventure on the wings of one whopper of a falsehood.

Why had we made the journey to such an out-of-the-way locale? What did we hope to accomplish there? Those questions and more swirled 'round in what I amusingly refer to as my brain as we were escorted into a common room and told that dinner would be served soon.

The common room was a large hall with immense wooden rafters that criss-crossed the high ceiling and oaken paneling that covered nearly every square inch of the walls. The smell of wood permeated the air, mixed with the scent of the oils no doubt used to keep it all in good repair and luster. I could very well believe that what I viewed was indeed a sailing vessel transformed into a home.

Lady Christmas announced my lady and me to the assembled guests who occupied the hall; our names caused no great stir, but I noted a few raised eyebrows over my companion's trousers. All-together, though, the Christmases' friends appeared to lean more toward the Bohemian than the dyed-in-the-wool blueblood.

Regardless, I realized immediately how under-dressed I was.

Walking into that room, I hoped that I did not appear too threadbare and patch-worked.

A sea of unfamiliar faces swept over me and I began to feel as if I was drowning after only a minute or so in the great hall. Snatches of conversation and the clinking of champagne glasses filled my ears to bursting and I tried to gravitate toward an outer wall and, perhaps, some fresh air not currently being used to gossip and schmooze.

Suddenly, I recognized a face, or thought that I did. A very popular jazz musician stood in the center of the room with a young woman of disreputable background hanging upon his arm – I was sure that it was he, for I had seen his face illustrated on the phonograph records of his that I owned. Biting my lip, I resisted the urge to engage the man in conversation and paint myself an utter fool by drooling in his drink. I hoped there might be time later on for such inanities.

I spotted my lady on the other side of the room and I watched as she strode through the crowd, her chin up and back erect, again looking nothing less than like a military man. A cold cloud descended upon me as I gazed at her; the feeling that she had changed, really *changed* since I first met her now quite strong. My lady looked both at home among the guests at Christmas Hall, but also somehow apart from them, a recognized authority figure yet one whom everyone is afraid to talk to.

There was no doubt in my mind that, if she so desired, she very well could pass herself off as Sgt. Janus' sister.

Whoever Sgt. Janus was, that is.

I checked my watch, wondered how long it would be until we could tie the old feedbag on, and then noticed a door to my left. On a whim, I opened the door and peered into the space beyond it. There, I could see a semi-lit corridor decorated in a very odd choice of wallpaper. Curious, I made my way through the door and shut it behind me, closing off all the unwelcome buzz of the guests of Christmas Hall.

I am no interior decorator, but the wallpaper in the corridor was definitely not one that I would have chosen, let alone understood.

The hallway stretched out only for about twenty feet or so and ended in a closed doorway. There were two paintings hung there on its walls, opposite each other, and two smallish chairs flanking a tiny little table on my right side as I faced the closed door. Overhead hung a medium-sized, semi-ornate chandelier. Very nondescript furnishings overall.

The wallpaper...how should I describe it? Vertical lines of faint gold ran through it, more or less spaced equally apart, but here and there the lines were crooked. Some of the lines continued from baseboard to the molding that separated the wall from the ceiling, but still others ended in small circles or, rarely, squares.

Simply looking at the pattern utterly confounded me. My brain tried to assign a name to the look of it, a country of origin for the pattern that might seem to make some sense of its seemingly random, higgledy-piggledy lines. But, ultimately, I could not guess at it. I began with the Asian world and moved on from there, but if the look fell within any ethnic sphere of design, I was at a loss to place it.

To further confuse the issue, I noticed that the wallpaper could only be seen from one direction.

As I walked the length of the corridor toward the door at the far end, I began to squint at the walls; within moments I realized the pattern was disappearing before my eyes, as well as changing from green to off-white. A most curious and alarming situation, I can assure you.

Then, reaching out with one hand to touch the wallpaper, I felt a most puzzling sensation. It was as if I had brushed up against something invisible and it immediately shied away from my touch.

That I did not call out aloud to my lady at that very moment is a testament to my growing acceptance of strange occurrences.

"Queer sort of paper, isn't it?" asked a pleasing voice in my ear. Already on edge I jumped, startled to find a pretty young lady standing at my elbow, smiling.

Apologizing for startling me, she introduced herself as Miss Gwendolyn Jackson, though, she insisted, her friends called her

Wendy. Then she also apologized for her intrusion.

Recovering quickly, I informed her that Mister J.M. Barrie had not done her full justice in his description of her in his famous story. To her credit, she did not titter, but simply smiled the more. The young lady did indeed remind me somewhat of her fictional counterpart, but far prettier.

We turned in unison to the wallpaper, each of us certain that the other was agreeable in discussing it. I liked her already.

"You think they know how godawful ugly it is?" I asked.

"Oh, certainly," said Wendy, brushing one shoulder against mine. "How could they not? Funny thing is that it's not repeated in any other part of Christmas Hall, so our hosts can't be all bad."

I began to ask her about mundane things like how long had she been at the Hall, who she was with; that sort of thing. It struck me as I listened to her answers that I seemed starved for another human being to talk to. The thought depressed me, despite Wendy's winning smile, her lovely long neck, and her slight scent of gardenia.

"Joshua?"

Yes, it would seem that my lot in life had become a tendency of Lady Janus to catch me talking with strange women.

"Ah, Wendy...err, Miss Gwendolyn Jackson, may I introduce you to my traveling companion...ahh, Lady Janus?"

I had expected the usual hackles raised over the appellation, or at least narrowed eyes over Wendy's comeliness, but to my surprise, warmth and animation flooded into my lady's frame.

"It's very fine to meet you, Miss Jackson," said she, stretching out one hand. "Are you here for the entire festive weekend?"

Suddenly, I was relegated to the background and couldn't get a word in edgewise. I slowed down, letting the two ladies move through the door and into the great hall. As I neared the doorway myself, I thought I heard something behind me.

Whispering.

Shutting the door, I paused, listened. The whispering stopped. I turned in place to take in the entire corridor, strange wallpaper and all. Then, almost inaudible, I could hear the sound of voices once more.

There was no mistaking it for the sound of insects or even the distinct hum of electric lights; though I couldn't make out any actual words, it had the cadence and structure of human speech.

My hand rose, unbidden, and reached out and away from me, my fingers feeling their way through the air of the corridor.

Someone called my name once again. I wheeled around to find my lady standing in the open doorway, one hand on the doorknob and one raised to crook a finger at me. I was needed, apparently.

I stepped over to her, blushing against my better judgment, but before either of us could speak, we heard a loud disturbance on the other side of the great hall.

Another guest had arrived.

Out in the entrance hall where we ourselves had arrived earlier, one voice rose over another, strident and angry.

"She said she was *who?*"

The other quieter voice was very obviously trying to placate the first, but in soft, assuring tones. I recognized it as that of Lord Christmas,' but the other sounded only vaguely familiar. Cutting in on our host, the louder voice rang out once again. A few of the guests turned toward it, mildly interested; I silently complimented them on their discretion.

"Never mind, Harry! I'll address this myself!"

Like an on-rushing crimson trolley car, Valerie Havelock-Mayer swept into the great hall, her eyes blazing like overloaded electric lamps.

She had changed little since we had least seen her, except perhaps she was more fiery, more beautiful, and most definitely more angry.

In a blur of red, Valerie catapulted herself across the room, dividing the throng of guests into two halves, and came to a stop only inches in front of my lady.

Why was it that all the attractive females in my adult life were of an odd, almost dangerous disposition?

My companion, God love her, said nothing. Her cool, detached gaze was a model for wealthy persons everywhere. I noted that though Valerie had a few inches on her, she appeared to be of equal height, just from her aloof manner alone.

"How dare you?" said Valerie Havelock-Mayer in an opening salvo.

Lady Janus inquired as to what she was presumably so daring about.

"Coming *here*," spat our scarlet friend, crossing her arms over her chest, "posing as...as *his* sister!"

Lady Janus widened her eyes ever so slightly. "I am here under no false pretenses, Madame Havelock-Mayer. If there are any misunderstandings, they rest not with myself, but with our host...and perhaps with *you*."

I thought it was an ill-advised comment that was sure to get us thrown out on our collective ear, but that surmise flew out the window when Valerie blanched at the words and abruptly drew her hand back, open-palmed. I tensed, ready to intervene.

"Ladies! Ladies!" Our Lord Christmas, finally showing some backbone.

All eyes went to the man. "Dinner is served!" he announced, smiling jovially.

We all filed into the dining hall, the battle postponed. War is hell, but apparently dinner is heaven.

Fortunately, Valerie Havelock-Mayer and her entourage were seated at the far end of the dining room from myself and my companion, though I could feel the woman's icy glare throughout our repast. It left me uneasy, a state I was rapidly becoming quite familiar with.

We were, interestingly, seated near our hosts, the Christmases, who took up residence at the head of our table and directed the serving of the meal by their servants. Next to me was my lady and next to her sat Miss Gwendolyn Jackson. I had almost forgotten the charming Wendy in the midst of the showdown out in the great hall, but after being seated and served a very nice Hungarian cucumber salad I relaxed a bit and managed to catch the pretty girl's eye. She smiled at me and then looked back to my lady, listening to something she'd been saying.

It was one of the more lively moments for Lady Janus that I'd yet witnessed.

Came the booming voice of Harry Christmas to disturb my reverie. "Why, yes," said our host to one of his guest's inquiry, "Christmas Hall is *inundated* with a long and rich history. Would you like to hear it?"

Everyone around us nodded their assent, myself included. Both Wendy and my lady turned their heads from their conversation to listen in also.

Christmas leaned over his plate, glancing around at those of us arrayed about him in an almost conspiratorial fashion. His wife suppressed a small smile, holding a napkin up over her lips.

"A ship's captain named Beryl Stokes," began our host, "who'd gained a rather sordid reputation on the high seas, had come into a goodly sum of exceedingly mysterious money late in his career; though he was never officially convicted of piracy. Stokes had a small fleet of corsairs that he operated in the 1790s, even supposedly did a bit of, ahem, *unspecified* work for the King of England..."

An older dowager across from me let out a gasp. "A *pirate*, you say?"

Lord Christmas grinned – clearly this was both a story he'd told many times and a reaction he relished. "Well, my dear, some say he may have *dabbled* in piracy now and then, but that's neither here nor there, for he amassed a small fortune *somehow*, and Old Beryl settled right *here*, about 1830 or so, and built this mansion."

"I've heard that he built it from his favorite ship or some such?" I asked.

"Quite," replied the man, "and the wood you see all around us once made up its hull and keel, its railing and masts..."

"Surely there's more wood in this structure than that which makes up even a large sailing ship?" That from Wendy, bless her. Clever, that one.

"Oh, uh, certainly, Miss Jackson," said Christmas behind a small, embarrassed-sounding cough. "But you must remember that this was all very long ago and stories can begin to change and..."

My lady spoke up then. "And his fortune? What became of it? Had he any family?"

The man brightened a bit, perhaps seeing a way back to his original tale-telling.

"No, Lady Janus, none at all. A bachelor his entire life, he spent his coin largely on himself and decorated this place with all sorts of exotic trappings from around the world; I'm sure you've already seen some of them. We've retained as much original furnishings as possible.

"And in answer to your question about his wealth, well, that's a mystery. After he settled here, Beryl Stokes had a theater built up in the city and some say that he hid the remainder of his ill-gotten gains in its vicinity. No one can truly say, because the pile's never been found."

Chewing on all of that, I opened my mouth once again. "Found a weird spot in a corridor, myself, right after we'd come in. Strange sort of wallpaper there…"

"Oh!" exclaimed Harry Christmas, making his wife jump. "That's the Whispering Wallpaper! Very good, Mr. Hargreaves; very good of you!"

Before I could ask for more details on my find, a large plate of steaming *coq au vin* was suddenly placed before me and my stomach bade me eat.

With the last remnants of a very fine cherry torte being cleared away by the servants and Turkish coffee offered in un-stingy amounts, I urged our host to tell me more of the so-called "Whispering Wallpaper."

"At one point," Christmas said, "not long before Captain Stokes died, a stranger showed up at his door and – here is where the story is somewhat muddled – somehow convinced the old seadog to allow him to run the estate. This man, whose very name has been lost in the mists of time, began to augment the already unusual collection of treasures here with even more strange artifacts from around the globe. That wallpaper you viewed in the corridor is a prime example of the man's handiwork. Odd, isn't it?"

I agreed that it was and asked him if he had determined its origin.

"No," he admitted, "not by half. Confounded me since the day I bought the place. And then the whispering began."

To this, my lady perked up. "Spirits?" she inquired, with a detachment which she believed hid the interest I knew brewed inside her.

Christmas crinkled his eyes at her. "Ghosts, you mean? Who can say, my dear lady; perhaps your brother could, eh?"

Someone in the room slammed a coffee cup down onto their table at that and I looked up to catch a fleeting glimpse of the departing red bustle of Valerie Havelock-Mayer. The two men who flanked her observed the growing stain of her jarred coffee on the tablecloth and then got up to rush out after her.

My lady threw down her napkin onto her dessert plate and, begging our pardons, got up and stalked off after the crimson fury.

It couldn't end well, no matter how I played the scenarios in my mind. I, too, begged the indulgence of my hosts and made my way into Lady Janus' wake.

A soft yet firm hand slipped into mine and I looked up to see Wendy at my side, one eyebrow arched in a way that seemed to ask me if the game was afoot.

Together, we hurried out into the great hall and into the maelstrom.

"I shall have you thrown out of this house...*bodily*," said Valerie Havelock-Mayer with a terse twist of her chin.

I rushed up to find the two opponents had resumed their face-off from before dinner. My lady stood with arms crossed and stroking her chin with one hand, her eyes observing the rich woman who maintained a distance of only inches from her. Valerie had positioned herself with hands on hips, her legs akimbo and her chest thrown out. It was all very *male*, I thought.

"I think not," said Lady Janus, coolly. "There may be some need for me here."

Valerie's quite lovely, yet cruel, eyes narrowed at that; evidently the comment touched upon more than one emotion behind them.

"*You*," she punctuated this with a pointed finger, "are *not* Roman Janus. I knew...*know* the man and you are not him. This...this *pretension* of adopting his name, living in his house...carrying out his-his *work*! It is beyond reason!"

To my surprise, before my companion could retort, Wendy released my hand and stepped up to the combatants and into Madame Havelock-Mayer's view.

"Valerie," she said, "this lady is a friend of mine. She is here because I invited her."

That was, of course, a lie, but what was one more when the entire weekend was built, one upon another, on them? The more important question coursing through my mind at that moment was to what end did Miss Jackson fib?

Valerie seemed blanched by the girl's comment. She opened her perfect scarlet lips to speak, but my new, most-favorite person on the Earth spoke again, cutting her off.

"And if I'm to understand Lady Christmas, it is *you* who are the gatecrasher here. I'm told you had no invitation to present."

Bully for Wendy! The barb inserted itself in our friend the saloon-keeper and stuck. Valerie pressed her eyes closed for a moment to collect herself and then spun on her heels, motioning to her two lackeys to leave the room ahead of her.

She stopped at the doorway. "This is far from over," said she, not turning to face us.

And then she was gone.

I walked over to my lady and gained her attention. "I can't fathom why you'd believe you were needed here. The whole thing's quite obviously a sham, the 'whispering wallpaper' and all that. Harry Christmas' little gambit to increase his business, to rope in the curious."

Yes, I heard the words I was saying, despite my encounter in the corridor. Still, I hoped I might sway my lady to pack up her kit and essay our departure before we had any more trouble out of that auburn-tressed demoness.

"A sham?" whispered my lady. "But...why? Why would someone *falsify* a haunting? I cannot credit it, Josuha..."

I could see her struggling with it, a conundrum without reason to her view of the universe. Instantly, I felt rotten for suggesting it; regardless, I spoke my mind again.

"Think about it. If Roman Janus had come here, perhaps even annually, wouldn't he have-have taken care of any *spirits*? Even with what little we know of him, I feel certain as to his integrity on these matters. *He* would have sussed out any ghouls or ghasts, I'm sure."

My lady had gained much strength since her acquisition of the disk from the Room of Visitation and I had seen in her a growing confidence. But at that time, she was clearly flummoxed.

My companion looked up at me, seeking something in my eyes and lightly and rhythmically thumping my chest with one closed fist, as if pounding out an answer to the dilemma. A small clearing of the throat then reminded us we were not alone.

"Miss Jackson, thank you." My lady was all cool and composed once more, her voice dropping an octave. "You are full of surprises."

Wendy bowed her head slightly, sketched a mock-curtsy. "Always wanted to give ol' Val the what-for. Her family and mine go a way's back, but rarely do we get a chance to put them in their place. Thank *you*...and goodnight."

She leaned in to softly brush her lips against my cheek. Then, after a second's consideration, stepped over to repeat the gesture on my companion.

The both of us stood there, shoulder to shoulder, watching as Wendy flew off and up the immense flight of stairs to the lodgings above.

Of course we returned later that evening to view the wallpaper. What do you take us for? Amateurs?

My lady and I met in the hallway outside our assigned rooms and silently made our way downstairs to the great hall. An old grandfather clock we passed told me it was almost midnight.

Christmas Hall took on a darker atmosphere at night and not just from the absence of light. Outside, I could see the surrounding forest through the windows and tried not to think of them as gigantic guardians of some occult significance. But it was difficult.

I opened the door to the corridor in question, held it open for my lady and once she was through, slipped past it myself and shut it firmly behind us. My companion turned up the chandelier via a dial set in the wall, but it failed to provide much illumination.

Thankfully, I had brought a small flashlight.

"Examine or listen?" I asked. My lady chose the former. We stepped closer to the paper and I flicked on my light.

"Most peculiar," she said, peering at the design. "Tribal, Joshua?"

"At a loss, I'm afraid. My schooling was somewhat expensive, but perhaps not all-inclusive. Just a country bumpkin at heart, I guess."

I found her eyes on me then, examining my face in lieu of the wallpaper. I reddened a bit, glad that the corridor was dim.

To my surprise she took my hand in hers.

"You've been a stalwart companion, Joshua. I couldn't ask for a better chronicler."

I smiled impulsively. "You've never read one single word I've written since you've known me," I reminded her.

"Be that as it may," my lady whispered through a suppressed smile of her own, "I..."

She squeezed my hand rather abruptly, crushing my fingers in her grip.

"Listen!" she hissed.

I listened.

Whispering.

"What is it *saying?*"

"Quiet," she urged. "Its most definitely words, but I cannot say whether it is English or not..."

As soon as the words had left my lady's lips, others came to my ear; directly into my ear, in fact.

"'Hate'," I told her.

My lady's eyes narrowed and her brow furrowed, a sure sign that we were getting somewhere.

"Is that what you heard?" she asked. "I believe I distinctly heard the word 'cell.'"

Dread crawled over me, cold and slimy. "Someone...someone is being held *captive?*"

My lady moved away from me and down the corridor toward the

far door. When she stopped and spoke again, the lack of good light, the distance, and her trousers made her look a man.

"This is wrong somehow. This doesn't feel *right*." She glanced back at me. "Does it feel wrong to you?"

Having very little experience in what constituted right or wrong in relation to spirits, I could only shrug my shoulders in ignorance, a gesture I'm sure my lady was becoming rapidly familiar with.

The whispering became louder. I too made out the word "cell."

Something brushed up against my arm and I spun around to find nothing or no one near me to cause such a sensation.

Then the lights went out completely.

"Spirits!" said Lady Janus in a loud voice that echoed around the corridor. "Spirits, attend me!"

I heard laughter, very softly but distinct, as if nearby. To my consternation, I could determine no source for it, no point of origin.

"They're playing with us," I told my lady.

"There *are* spirits that derive a kind of joy from confusing the living," she returned.

Just as mysteriously as they arrived, the whisperings then departed. We stood there for many more minutes but determined that the night held no more enigmas for us. We agreed to return to our rooms and reconvene over the matter in the morning.

Something touched my neck on our way out of the corridor.

I thought that Wendy might have a good chuckle over our little escapade the night before, but she listened to my account of it with interest and I could see her sluicing the bits of it in her mind, looking for nuggets of gold.

"Can I go with you tonight, then?"

The thought hadn't occurred to me that she'd be interested in doing any such thing, let alone that my lady and I would return for another evening's vigil over the wallpaper. I told Wendy that wasn't the only member of the team; we'd have to put it to the lead investigator.

"Absolutely not," said the lady in question as she took her spot at the breakfast table. "The more living persons in attendance, the less likely there will be a spirit presence. It's a proven fact."

I wanted to ask where she got such a "fact," but knew better than to bother. Wendy pouted prettily and asked me to regale her again with the particulars of our first vigil. This was interrupted by a small procession through the dining area by Valerie Havelock-Mayer and her lackeys. Interestingly, Valerie gave my lady no look, not even a hint of a glance, and moved along with a sort of satisfied or smug expression on her beautiful face.

It should have bothered me, gnawed at me, but Wendy's eager interest in the case dispelled any gloom I might have felt from both our adversary and the previous evening's feelings of dread.

In fact, the girl bolstered my, ahem, spirits and that served me well much later when the clock once again struck midnight and Lady Janus and I were once again on the prowl.

As I shut the door behind us, I sensed immediately the different feeling that hung over the corridor, different from the previous night. Then, my lady felt that something was wrong; now I felt it too.

We decided to listen first, and if that failed us, to try and communicate with the spirit or spirits.

"Spirit, we are here," announced my companion. "How many of you are there? Are you in pain? In torment of some kind?"

Whispering once more, yet the timbre of it had changed. I was certain that it was a male voice, whereas before I could not say that with certainty. My lady agreed with my assessment.

I noticed that she kept one hand in her coat pocket.

Then, a low moan filtered into the area and more words. Either the haunting was escalating due to our presence, or…

"To where does this corridor lead?" I asked, but not of the spirits.

"My thought precisely, Joshua," answered my companion. "Do you have your pistol with you?"

I smiled at the familiar question, but admitted that I had left it in my room; what was a pistol against the supernatural? I felt charged up, though, and, taking her by the arm we turned and marched down the corridor to its far end.

The moaning and whispering followed us, now suffused with a buzzing giggle.

Approaching the door at the corridor's end, I kicked it open with my foot. Beyond was another hallway, but running perpendicular to the one we had just exited. The whispering stopped at the precise moment I crashed through the door, to be replaced with louder voices of alarm coming from my left.

I leapt toward the voices to find a small anteroom that bordered the Whispering Wallpaper corridor and therein three men, crouching against the wall in the darkness, the smell of spirits permeating the space.

I couldn't see their faces clearly, but I could discern their surprise, their drunkenness, and the odd metal horns they held up against the wall.

"Hey!" I shouted, at a loss for anything else to say. My anger had overridden my ability to write dialogue, I guess. It turned to look at Lady Janus, expecting anger there, too, but finding a more controlled version of it, laced with loathing.

"You *fiends...*" she muttered, balling her hands into fists.

One of the men got up off his knees, shakily, and advanced on us.

"Here now, this...this a *private* party...yes," he slurred. "Take your little *piece* here, boy, and plumb 'er summer else!"

"Monsters," seethed my lady. "*Who* has put you up to this? You haven't enough brains among the lot of you to assemble it on your own!"

Well, that did it. The man charged us, bellowing inarticulate sounds.

My lady and I reacted at the very same time. We flanked the man on both sides, more or less, and at the precise moment she stuck out a foot to trip him, I lashed out with a fist and caught him in the side of the head as he began to fall to the floor.

Something metallic struck me on the shoulder then, and I looked up to see another of the men barreling toward me. He caught me

around the midsection with a mighty crash and we went down together, sprawling over his prone partner-in-crime.

"Run!" I shouted to Lady Janus as fists pummeled me in the
darkness. There was barely any room for me to swing back, but I intended to give as good as I got, peaceable sort that I am. My knuckles found some soft surfaces and I put all I had behind them.

Thank goodness my opponent was fairly shickered.

Something suddenly crashed down on his bullet head. He fell
off me and I looked up to see my companion tossing to one side the
remains of a chair. As one, we turned to the third man.

"I give up," he announced, slumping back against the wall. "Had
enough. Don' wan' no more. She can keep 'er money…"

That was when Valerie Havelock-Mayer chose to arrive on the
scene. Funny how these things happen.

"What is going on here?"

"No need to act so bewildered, Valerie," said my lady. "We know
that it was you who paid these men to falsify the haunting."

Madame gave no retort. She stood there, hands at her sides, a
silhouette in the darkness. Overall, from what I could see, she appeared rather well-composed for someone who might have been
woken up by loud noises and decided to investigate.

Of course, the wealthy always look good, I suppose.

Illumination spread through the area, suddenly. I looked over to
see Wendy Jackson at a light switch, a thousand questions on her face.

She rushed over and flung her arms about me and asked me if
I were all right. It was hard to concentrate on her, though I would
have liked to; I was too busy watching my lady and Valerie.

"You had us followed here." It was a statement, not a question.
My companion was very sure in what she was saying.

"You knew that we would receive an invitation for this weekend
here at Christmas Hall," she continued, "and you hoped we would
attend. Perhaps it occurred to you that it would make for an opportunity to confront me? To…'expose' me?"

"Yes," replied Valerie, plainly, without subterfuge. I noticed that while her face was impassive, her right hand trembled.

Lady Janus gestured toward our three assailants.

"These men have not served you well, Valerie."

"No, they haven't," came the swift reply. The woman's voice was less sure now; I believed I heard a crack run through it. Her trembling hand was now balled into a fist.

My dark lady spread her own hands wide. "What do you want from me, Valerie?"

The woman in red stepped toward her; I tensed, ready to spring to my lady's defense.

"I want," said Valerie, now visibly shaking, "I want...to know... *the truth!*"

"This is the truth." My lady indicated herself, one hand upon her breastbone.

Madame Havelock-Mayer took another step, coming closer to my lady.

"Tell me *where* Roman Janus is. Tell me what...has *happened...* to him!"

With that she sprung, her fists raised and ready to strike. My lady caught her wrists with sure hands and held the woman back. Hot tears streamed down from Valerie's face, her mouth twisted into a horrible shape.

"You are a *charlatan!*" she screamed, trying to wrestle out of my lady's grip. "Just as *he* was! Oh, God ... *tell me where he is!*"

Lady Janus did not release her, but through some strange force of will brought the hysterical woman back from the brink and quieted her.

Then they locked eyes for a long, long moment.

"Oh, Lord," whispered Valerie Havelock-Mayer. "No..."

She broke away and, cradling the shreds of her dignity, removed herself from the room.

I sent my companion back to her room, despite her protests to the contrary. That left me alone with Wendy.

"So, Valerie wanted to, what? Create fake ghosts and then try to show everyone here that Lady Janus was a fake herself?"

"Something like that, I suspect." I was tired and confused, not really in the mood for more talking.

Wendy leaned in to me, her face only inches from mine. "I'm so very glad you weren't hurt, or not very much hurt."

She put her soft lips to my cheek and then to my own lips. I wanted to melt into her kiss, let it obscure the damage of the evening…but something nagged at me.

Gently, very gently, I pushed Wendy away from me, so I could see her face.

"You know," I told her, "it occurs to me that Valerie's men arrived here before her, after they had reported that we were on our way here to Christmas Hall. Probably got here before us. But they didn't have invitations, most likely."

She looked at me curiously, not speaking.

"Someone who was already here," I explained, "would have had to let them in."

Wendy frowned. She then got up and walked to the doorway, her back to me.

"Why?" I asked her, suddenly feeling very, very sick.

"Family connections, you know," she said. "That sort of thing. You wouldn't understand, not really."

"But the time you confronted Valerie? Came to Lady Janus' defense?"

Wendy spun around to look at me, a slight smile on her lips. "Oh, that. That was real. Like I said, we Jacksons get so few opportunities to fight back."

She turned to leave, but before she disappeared, she glanced over her shoulder at me, her pretty eyes sad.

"I do like you, Joshua. That's real, too. And I'm sorry."

Here's my theory. I formed it as we drove away from Christmas Hall and back to Janus House. Amazing what the wind in your face does to aide your thoughts.

It was real.

The ham-handed haunting of the inebriated lackeys was a joke. But, the whispering I heard *before* all that, and the times that I felt I was touching something or something was touching me? That was real.

But it wasn't ghosts. There were no spirits. Not really.

Bear with me on this, I beg of you. It came together slowly in my mind and even after it had more fully formed as a theory, it is still most incredible.

And troubling. Exceedingly troubling.

After the fight, after the shocking sight of Valerie Havelock-Mayer's pleas, and after Wendy's betrayal, I could not fathom the thought of sleep. I returned to the corridor of the Whispering Wallpaper and, securing a comfortable chair, I sat down for a long visit.

I heard things that night. I heard more whisperings, more words...even a few sentences. I divined a *presence* there.

I am no Spirit-Breaker. I leave that to my dark lady. But I am something of a thinker, given half a chance, and what I think is this:

What I heard was not the past. It was the future.

This idea came to me as I listened to the voices and stared at the wallpaper. A connection of a sort was made in my head, not unlike when we turn on the electric lights. In fact, that thought helped me to form my theory, incredible as it may sound.

When I heard the phrase, "I hate my cell," I at first surmised that I was privy to the plea of a prisoner, but upon further attentive listening, and even meditation, I realized that it meant something else. Something *different*.

I was listening to the future. And, perhaps, it was listening to *me*.

Which means, according to my theory, that I am dead to those who occupy that future. I am the ghost. I am the spirit.

Even bearing that troubling idea, I managed to return us to Janus House in one piece. Again, we said little to each other along the way, and I did not share my theory with my lady.

Almost as soon as we stepped over the threshold, she made excuses to rush off. Damn me, but I followed her.

She, of course, made her way to the forbidden door and entered it.

I, with my thoughts, returned to my own room.

Interlude over Biscuits

The breakfast table is not the best place to have a discussion about spirits, perhaps, but I'd been perusing the library again and after a pleasant hour or so with a holiday classic, I had a burning question on my mind.

"Did Dickens have it right?" I inquired, stabbing at the air with a glob of preserves on my knife for emphasis.

My companion looked up at me from across the table. "Beg pardon? Did he have what right? And why are you reading Christmas stories at this time of year?"

"The Ghosts, of course," I replied, ignoring that last question. "Past, Present, Future, all that. They hardly seem the sort we've encountered. Was he being fanciful? Or are there such higher forms of spirits?"

"Let's just say that Mr. Dickens had a singular way with words and leave it at that."

Undeterred, I forged ahead. "No, I mean it: Are there spirits like the ones he described? His seem almost a force unto themselves, hardly the type to have had previous mortal lives."

That one took hold and my companion eyed me with some minor annoyance.

"No, or at least not in my experience. Those which the man told of in his overly-sentimental bit of tripe were akin to *angels* or some other heavenly servants than true ghosts – that is, the spirits of the human dead. I wouldn't trust Dickens for honest reporting; it's likely there was more absinthe to it than ectoplasm."

I thought I had already experienced much in my young life, but coming across someone who actually did not care for *A Christmas Carol* was a startling revelation to me – especially over breakfast.

Glutton for punishment that I am, I pressed on.

"We are only to credit the image of Jacob Marley then?"

"Yes, actually," admitted my companion. "That *is* a fairly good fictional representation of a true spirit, which you should well know by now. The amount of chains was a bit much, but the suffering appearance and the wailing – not to mention the warning of post-death punishment – are all within reason."

I smiled. "Then God bless us, every one, Dickens isn't a complete waste."

"No, in fact, as a sleeping draught I find him very effective."

Well, very little can drain me of the Christmas spirit, even "at this time of year," but my companion gave it the old college try. I sat quietly for a moment or three, rallying my forces and aligning my final salvo.

"If you had to say," I asked carefully, "whether or not a man like Scrooge could ever do enough in life to save him from the yawning pits of Hell in the afterlife, how might you opine?"

Incredibly enough, I was met with eyes not shooting daggers, but with an odd wistfulness that belied the early part of the conversation.

"There your writer does impart some small, valuable nuggets of wisdom," came the reply in even tones. "The lesson of Ebenezer Scrooge is that we may indeed atone for much before the grave, and help to insure an eternal rest with the Creator after."

Satisfied that we had come full circle and that Charles Dickens' legacy remained intact, I returned to my breakfast with gusto.

"Merry Christmas," I whispered around bites of biscuit.

"Might I suggest," offered my companion just then, "that you also pose the same question to our guest?"

"Guest?"

"Yes, the one standing right there at your elbow. Go on, ask him."

"Oh, come now! Must you? *I haven't even finished my breakfast yet!*"

This House Rag
By J. Hargreaves

The house is never quiet
There's always something jumpin' up
The house is nearly empty
So who did break my lovin' cup?

I can never get my rest
There's always some spirit on the step
I can never feel alone
When I can always feel them in my bones

The house is always noisy
There's never a break from the sound
The house is always pumpin'
But why's there no marks on the ground?

I can never get my rest
There's always some spirit on the step
I can never feel alone
When I can always feel them in my bones

This house never lifts me up
There's usually somethin' bringin' me down
This house is full of bangers
Oh, how I wish they'd stop hangin' 'round!

I can never get my rest
There's always some spirit on the step
I can never feel alone
When they always want my bones!

Chapter V
MARCHING TO PERDITION

I was lost.

It had begun to occur with some regularity; I would leave my own room at sprawling Janus House and then find myself lost in its warren of hallways.

The first time I credited the phenomenon to a lack of decent sleep or perhaps even a simple case of allowing my mind to wander, but on the second occurrence I sensed that something wasn't right. I knew damn well how to get from my room to the kitchens or the dining hall or the study, and I damn well wasn't growing senile.

It happened for a third time and after that I was aware of a *power* of some sort, almost as if the house was rearranging itself to create a path for me. Something was working behind the scenes to lead me astray

Or to lead me to a predestined location within the house.

On the fourth occurrence I found myself very near the door I was forbidden to open. Dread spread out and over me as I looked at the door, not daring to reach out and take hold of its knob, but desperately wanting to ... if only to end the long charade between my lady and me over its closed state.

I hurried away from the door, not trusting myself. Once I had turned the corner in the corridor, I heard the sound of the door opening and closing and then footsteps coming closer. Quickly, I turned myself around so to make it appear as if I was approaching the area rather than fleeing it.

Of course it was Lady Janus. She looked up at me with serious eyes and informed me that she would like to go for a drive. Would I care to humor her request? I said that I would be honored and we loaded into the Lincoln and were off within a matter of minutes.

Before we had left, I put the top up on the automobile, for it looked like rain.

My lady settled herself beside me on the seat, all done up in a tweed suit, longcoat, and with a cap on her head underneath which she had stuffed her long, raven hair. This affectation had become something of a habit for her since our last adventure. Sadly, I was witnessing the last dregs of her femininity fall away to be replaced by a more staid persona. My lady carried herself quite differently now.

As we sped away from Janus House and Mount Airy, she direct-ed me to drive westward, despite the nasty, angry storm clouds that were gathering there in the sky. I figured we'd meet them before long and was glad I'd put the top up.

With a few miles behind us, I was wondering to myself whether it was to be another ride about the countryside in mutual silence when my lady surprised me by speaking.

"Joshua," she said, "I know we've had a rough patch or two, but I assure you that I am indeed feeling very strong now. Those moments of...weakness are behind me. I'm much more myself these days and would like to try and resume my full activities."

That inspired a hot flash of anger in me and I bit down on my tongue until I could stand it no longer; I made up my mind there and then to let her have a significant piece of it.

Suddenly, a signpost appeared up ahead of us and my attention wandered toward it. It read "Pitcairn."

I realized I was lost again.

We continued to drive for several more miles, passing around and through a string of little towns with names like "Porten," "Samovar," "Raleighsburg," and "Casperinius." I asked my lady if she cared to stop in one of them so that I might gather my wits and get us back on to a major thoroughfare, but a flash of lightning and a peal of thunder heralded an impromptu course change.

At a little wooden sign by the side of the road that pointed to "Hope's Puddle" some three miles to the north, my lady suddenly shouted for me to turn the motorcar toward it.

Fighting to keep us upright, I made the turn and we resumed our speed, heading in the direction of either fate or foolishness, but more than likely given our recent history, a bit of both.

Drops of rain, heavy and wet, began to fall from the grey sky above as I slowed down and came to a stop by a nearly-invisible turn-off. Following my lady's pointing finger, I could make out the dirt road she indicated. Sighing, I peered up at the growing storm and turned the Lincoln onto the uneven and potted path.

After only a half-mile or so a building appeared out of the deluge before us.

I let my foot off the accelerator and allowed the bumpy dirt road to act as a kind of natural brake. The rain was falling in sheets by then, creating watery curtains that danced before our eyes. I resisted the urge to wipe imaginary water from my face; we were still dry within the automobile.

The structure looked like a small farmhouse. Two stories tall and with a single chimney, it faded in and out of my field of vision, grey and watery as its surroundings. My lady leaned forward on the seat, gazing through the slick windshield with interest at the house.

Then, before my eyes, it ghosted away from view, completely disappearing into the downpour.

I must have exclaimed out loud, a wordless expression of my surprise, for my dark lady reached out and patted my arm, perhaps to assure me that she too had seen what I had seen.

Compelled to prove to myself that I *had* seen the house, I stepped out of the Lincoln and saw that the space in front of us held nothing more than the remains of a foundation; a large hole in the ground that was rapidly filling up with water.

My lady came up from behind me and stood at my side to view the hole. The rain fell steadily for a minute more and then lessened enough for us to see another depression in the ground some feet beyond the house foundation. I guessed it to be where a barn might have once stood. It was partially caved in and grown over with grass and weeds, so I assumed the original structure that stood on the spot had been gone longer than the presumed farmhouse.

A figure walked towards us through the rain, denying us any detail until it came within twenty feet or so of our position. It stood there silently for a moment, looking at us, then doffed its hat.

It was a woman; she might have been thirty or thereabouts, pretty but careworn.

"Well," she said finally, "you've come. It's about time."

After apologizing to us for her rudeness, the woman introduced herself as Dorothy St. George. Upon closer inspection, I saw that she was indeed handsome, but her face had been prematurely lined by some tragedy or other extreme hardship.

She invited us to come in and before I could point out that there was no "in" to go to, my lady and I were ushered into a small wooden cabin that sat beyond what was once a farmstead, I supposed. Thankfully, the cabin was warm and cheery inside, filled with the welcome smell of a cooking roast and vegetables heavily doused with basil and thyme.

Therein we met Dorothy's husband Richard, who also looked a bit older than his years, but not quite so much as his wife. He got up to greet us politely enough, but there was caution, a wariness in his carriage that I made a mental note of.

My lady removed her hat and shook out her long black locks and received a look of surprise from both the St. Georges.

"But-but I don't understand…" said Dorothy, looking back and forth from my lady and myself. Quickly, I introduced myself to perhaps give my companion a moment to think. Of course, she needed none such saving, for she stepped boldly forward, extended her hand in proper fashion and identified herself simply as "Janus."

Our hostess, after a moment of awkward silence in which she scrutinized my lady's face, recovered well and invited us to sit at her table for dinner. Richard also studied my lady silently as his wife moved about the kitchen area and began to tell us her ghost story.

Seems that almost exactly a year before, Dorothy was alone for a week in the farmhouse that once stood on the empty foundation and, deluged by rain that she claimed never let up, became inundated by spirits, one after another, seven in all.

It was plain to me then that whatever truly happened in the house had been responsible for the stress and strain that had taken their toll on her. I felt for her; it must've been a horrible experience.

Richard added a bit at the end about how he found her when he'd returned from his business trip and together they decided to have the house pulled down; whatever had happened there was apparently too much for them both to bear. Now, the little cabin in which we sat was there only abode, something new and wholly theirs.

Dorothy also explained that she had written up the entire adventure and mailed it off to Janus House in hopes that she might clear up a few of that arduous week's mysteries.

"I'm certain that it was Sgt. Janus who came to my rescue," I remember her saying with conviction and passion. "I don't know how or even why, but the image of his face is burned into my memory… as well as the faces of those-those…things that visited me."

"It's not terribly unusual," Lady Janus noted, "for spirits to appear in progression, especially in sevens. In your case, something of their regimented lives carried over into their after-lives. You say that they appeared to you as a troop of soldiers?"

Dorothy nodded, staring at my lady and mechanically folding and refolding a small towel, over and over again.

"Well, then, that explains it."

She said it so damned matter-of-factly that it made me want to scream at her that these people were victims of *something* and needed consolation and understanding, not a cold affirmation of spirit movements.

Instead I asked her about the image of the house we'd seen when we arrived.

"Oh, that," she said, turning to me. "Yes, now *that's* somewhat unusual. A spirit structure."

Forgetting for a moment all that I'd encountered since being Lady Janus' "chronicler," I sputtered my disbelief.

"A ghost house? Surely a *house* doesn't have a...a *spirit*, too? It's not a living thing!"

"No," she said calmly, "not in the sense that we humans are akin to, but houses and other sorts of buildings create a kind of a 'web of life' while they stand and there have been instances of their spirit forms manifesting after they've been torn down. I believe Mrs. St. George here has offered credible evidence for the house to have been a focal point for para-normal activity, which goes to illustrate its current spirit presence."

She asked Richard if he knew much of the house's history. He admitted that he didn't and that when he had bought it the land agent claimed he knew little himself.

My lady stood up and walked toward the door without saying another word. I knew enough by then of her strange habits that I followed without question.

For several minutes she walked about the foundation of the former farmhouse and the barn that once sat alongside it. Then breaking her reverie, she called out to Dorothy to indicate from which direction the first spirit had approached, and our hostess pointed to the fields to the west of the property. My lady nodded at that, then went back to her walking and thinking.

The rain had stopped by then, thank goodness, but the skies remained dark and troubled. I'd always liked rain, honestly, and looked forward to that exhilarated feeling one gets when a storm rolls in, but that sky was nothing I cared for. It was the dictionary definition of ominous.

My lady only added to that dread when she finally ceased her pacing about and returned to the cabin.

"I believe everything you have told us," she said to our hosts, "but there are many things I still don't understand. I do know, though, that it isn't over."

Dorothy went white and clutched her husband's arm.

"What you experienced was only a first sortie," my lady explained.

"They will be back and soon. And we must be prepared for them."

I went back outside and stood away from the cabin, underneath a great old pine tree. The rain had stopped, but the sky continued to grumble and groan with thunder somewhere off in the distance. I suddenly hoped there might still be a chance that we could wrap up the whole thing quickly and move along.

My dark lady had a differing opinion to mine.

She appeared at my side and gazed out over the landscape with me. After a long quiet moment, she spoke of having to "purify and clarify" herself for the coming task. I inquired as to what that entailed and she replied that it was much too lengthy a process to go into. Perhaps it was the mood I was in at the time, but it sounded like a lot of mumbo-jumbo to me.

"Joshua," she said, forcing me to face her and look her in the eye, "please don't do anything stupid. I need you in this."

I told her I couldn't promise I wouldn't do anything particularly stupid and would try to hold my overall inanities down to a dull roar.

And with that she was gone, I knew not where.

"I hope you don't mind my saying, but she's an odd one."

It was Richard St. George, stepping beneath the tree and removing a cigarette from a case to light. He didn't offer me one.

"I sort of do mind," I told him, "but feel powerless to do anything about it. Haven't the spirit at the moment."

He grunted. "Spirits. Funny business, that. How long have you been in it?"

"Too long, apparently."

He flicked ash from his cigarette and turned to me. "Listen, Hargreaves; I don't truck with all this, not really, but Dorothy believes in it and she had a pretty bad time a year ago. I pulled down a perfectly good house to calm her mind, but I'm not prepared to go much beyond that. I'd appreciate it if you could ask this-this *Janus* to not encourage Dorothy." He grimaced. "We were just starting to come out of it."

I smiled, but without mirth. "I don't hold her leash, sir. I...I don't do much of anything, to be frank about it. The lady does as she will and…and I've seen her actually *help* people."

"Do *you* believe in it all?" he asked, his manner intensifying.

I turned to go, having my fill of the man and his unspoken accusations.

"Not sure what I believe, but I'm in it for the long haul," I threw over my shoulder. "You watch yours, I'll watch mine."

I walked away from the encounter furious, both at myself and my lady, and unsure of what was to come next. Something had to give, that much I knew at least.

Through the mist I spied the tall structure of a windmill and made my way over to it. Looking up to its top, some fifty or more feet above the ground I judged, it occurred to me that I could see for miles around by climbing it.

It was the stupidest thing I could think of in a pinch.

My head filled with questions as to what exactly was to be "purified" and "clarified," I began my assent. The going was fairly easy and I made good time; within minutes I was at the top and looking between the blades of the windmill to view the rain-soaked countryside.

Finding the foundation of the original house, I recalled what Dorothy had said about the direction from which the spirits in her tale had approached and oriented myself. Following a line from where I believed she stood at the window a year ago, I saw wide fields that seemed to stretch off into the distance and meet with the troubled sky at the horizon. Despite the threatening clouds and the moisture still in the air, it was all somewhat beautiful.

I sat on my perch for a long time, allowing my anger to boil off. The day came and went and finally night arrived and the air grew exceedingly chilly. I wondered what those on the ground were doing and made up my mind to return to the soil once more.

I had just begun to take my first step in lowering myself when something out in the fields caught my eye.

A figure.

I blinked, wiped at my eyes, and it was gone.

After a few more steps downward, I dared to look out at the fields again. There stood the figure, as clear as clear.

I yelled, an inarticulate shout with no real reasoning behind it. The blades of the windmill turned just then, perhaps loosened from my shout, and passed in front of me. When one blade had cleared my vision, I saw that the figure had disappeared.

Angry again, I continued my descent. When I came within ten feet or so from the ground, I looked again.

The figure stood some one-hundred yards from me, glowering and glowing with a sickly, pale green light.

Startled, I missed a handhold and fell.

Time passed, as it does, but did so without my recognition. I awoke some time later with no accounting as to how long I had been unconscious.

The first thing I saw when I opened my eyes was a face, hovering over mine. I did not recognize it, so I recoiled from it. Then I felt the rather intense pain in my leg.

"Joshua, thank the Lord!" exclaimed the face. I thought the voice familiar but still it did not register in my memory. My eyes were rheumy and unclear. I wiped at them with one hand.

I saw then that the face belonged to my companion, she who I called Lady Janus.

Her long, dark, raven hair had been cut short, to the extent that she looked as if she was ready to join the ranks of some branch of the military. She had also bleached it to a sandy blonde hue. Her face was gaunt…no, that's not entirely accurate. Say more…angular or stony, more like a man's features than those of the beautiful woman I had followed now for months. In her right ear she wore a small band of copper.

It was a disturbing picture to awaken to.

I asked how long I'd slept. My lady informed me I'd been out for two whole days. I asked then why my leg was in such pain.

Another face appeared. It was Dorothy St. George, smiling shyly and quite obviously distraught.

"It's broken," she said. "Badly, I'm afraid. You're running a fever."

I did feel hot just then, despite cool breezes that wafted in from the window by my bed. Suddenly, I smelled rain and then heard the soft patter of raindrops.

"Yes," my lady said, nodding to my unspoken question. "The entire time. They are coming nearer."

"Like before," whispered Dorothy, frowning.

My anger over my leg overwhelmed my curiosity over the rain, though.

"Why haven't you set my leg?" I demanded, which sent a sharp spike of new pain through it. "I don't want to be lame for the rest of my life!"

Yes, I was shaken, shaken soundly, and though it was my own fault that I climbed that tower, fear loosened my tongue and I spoke harshly.

My lady appeared sheepish, turning her eyes downward. Dorothy put a hand on her shoulder, but my companion shied away from it. I looked back and forth between the two of them, searching their faces for an answer.

"We…we couldn't," replied Dorothy, finally. "I have no experience in that area. I could have made it worse."

Furious, I turned to my lady, tried to sit up. My leg screamed for me to be still, but I was frantic at the moment.

"As could I," she said soberly. "I have no medical abilities, Joshua. The break is a bad one, as Dorothy said, and…"

She was lying. Bald-faced lying! What else could it be? I saw her attend to Judge Holding back in Canal Chichester; I guessed then that she'd been a nurse, so sure and proficient was she in her care and handling of the man.

In spite of my fever, I shivered. She'd gone off two days ago for some sort of half-baked "purification" ritual and returned as the stranger that sat next to me on the bed and told me, in so many words, that she wasn't who I thought she was. Something had changed again, and I saw the last vestiges of "my lady" slipping away. Even the usual scent of lavender was gone from her.

"And you are?" I asked, as I had asked her all those months ago in my little hometown.

She looked up at me with queer eyes, green and splintered rather than the gun-metal blue I had become accustomed to.

"Janus," she said with smooth confidence.

Gathering up my wits I asked why one of them hadn't taken the motorcar and fetched a doctor? Surely there was one somewhere in the area?

"I only recently returned to the cabin, Joshua," said Janus. "The rain has been quite heavy at times. Mrs. St. George has been caring for you, watching over you."

I realized then that Richard St. George was not in the room. I inquired as to his whereabouts.

"Gone," answered Dorothy, wringing her hands. "He walked out of here yesterday and hasn't returned. Oh, he takes long walks sometimes, but this…is unusual."

With nothing to hide, I told her that Richard and I had had words shortly before I climbed the tower and that he wasn't terribly fond of my and my companion's presence. The woman nodded at that, and in doing so clearly explained that she and her husband were not of the same mind on spirits and hauntings.

"Well, I'm awake now. Feel like I've been mauled by bears, but at least I'm up. Can't *someone* go for a doctor now?"

Janus asked Dorothy if she could drive an automobile and when she answered in the affirmative implored her to take the Lincoln and fetch a surgeon post haste.

"I must stay here," she explained. "I'm needed."

"Yes," I grunted, "if only to take care of the nasty-looking chap that made me fall off the tower."

Janus' eyes widened and she reached out to grab me by the shirt front. "What?" she yelped. "Joshua…you *saw* one of them? *Here*, near the cabin?"

I screamed in pain. Her jostling of me shifted my leg and I almost fainted from the agony of the broken bone.

"I'm sorry," she soothed, "I'm sorry, Joshua." Whipping around to look at Dorothy, she extended one index finger and pointed toward our automobile.

"Go! Get a doctor! *They* are coming, and coming *soon*! And this time they will try to finish the work they started a year ago!"

A thunderclap punctuated her command, and the rain fell heavily on the little cabin as the skies darkened to almost night.

Dorothy grabbed a shawl from the back of a chair and a small bag and promised she'd be back as soon as possible. She paused then and looked back at Janus and me, an odd expression on her face.

"I-I feel like I *know* you both, trust you," she said, tears in her eyes. "Please, be safe. And please let Richard know that I'm not angry with him."

With that she was gone. Without hesitation, my companion tore away the curtains that hung over the window near my bed, providing us both with a clear, unobstructed view of the surroundings including the wide expanse of fields that held dark portent for the coming hours.

We saw Dorothy get in the Lincoln and after a brief moment of familiarizing herself with it, she started it up and pulled away. The rain came down even harder, as if to express its ire over her departure.

I turned to the woman who remained with me, studied her once more.

"All purified and clarified, are we?"

"Let's have none of that," she said, but not harshly. "This isn't some simple spirit manifestation, Joshua. No ghost in an old rectory, or faint knockings in the wainscoting. This is likely a major push for them, a major *offensive*..."

I tried to sit up again, but gingerly. "You speak as if it were a military thing," I told her through gritted teeth.

"It *is*," she hissed, skewering me with a pointed look. "That's exactly what it is. The St. Georges found themselves in the path of a military operation last year. These...*soldiers* want something here on the grounds…or they simply want the current landowners *off* these grounds. I'm not certain which. Not yet."

I thought back over Dorothy's recounting of her arduous experience all those months ago.

"What do you make of that *word* she heard, in her basement?"

Janus stopped moving about the room, but did not look at me again.

"Again, I'm not certain," she replied, staring off into the fields, "but I feel as if it were a…secret password or some such. The spirit that spoke it might have been waiting for a reply."

I considered that, still studying my companion's form. "Funny that, that she couldn't even *repeat* it to us…"

"Yes," said Janus, "but as I've told you before, words and names hold immense power and this one in particular must be. Hello, what's *this?*"

Startled, I swung my head around to try and see what she had seen out the window. There, a short distance from the cabin, in the middle of the tall grass, something moved.

I peered at the shape, trying not to shift my leg. At first I thought it to be a large, dark rock that sat on the property, but I could see it move slightly at first, then vibrated more fully.

The thing stood up suddenly. It was a man.

Lightning flashed, illuminating the man's features in the rain-soaked atmosphere.

It was Richard St. George.

He began to move toward the cabin with shaky, unsure steps. They reminded me of those of a toddler, still learning to walk.

"Lock the door," I said.

Janus was already on it, exiting the room and moving toward the outer door of the cabin. I heard her turn its lock and set the bar across it. Returning to the bedroom, we listened as Richard tried the door and, finding it barred, seemingly moved away.

"Are we doing the right thing?" I asked. "It is, after all, *his* home."

My companion shook her head, studying the window. "Yes, but something isn't right. Until we can determine what he's about, we must…"

A dark from appeared at the window: Richard.

Instinctively, I threw up my blanket and covered my head and face. Glass shattered and fell all about me. A frigid wind whipped into the room and stirred all the things that occupied it.

I looked to see Richard St. George still standing at the window, but now his shirtsleeves were in tatters and blood ran down his forearms and hands. I could barely see his face, but his eyes seemed to glow in the darkness.

"What do you want?" demanded Janus in a strong, commanding voice. I rallied at the sound of it. "Speak!"

Richard opened his mouth and uttered a single word.

"*Stenndec...*"

I found it to be almost impossible to type out here, long after the fact. I wholeheartedly believe Dorothy St. George and her own struggles with it; I swear it is of the devil, or maybe even beyond even that. It chills me to even think of it, so insidious is it in my brain.

Janus flinched, but held her ground. I could see the word had an effect on her, too, but not as strongly as on me.

"*What do you want?*" she bellowed, stepping toward the window, her shoes crunching the broken glass littered across the floor.

Richard looked at me. "See you've taken a spill. Serves you right, playing the hero."

His voice contained a strange quality, one that I had not heard in it before. My mind whirled with thoughts, most of them of how to move away from the man at the window.

Swinging one leg up and over the windowsill, he stumbled over it and crashed to the floor in a heap. I began to move off the bed, though my leg screeched at me to stop. The pain was so intense, I thought I'd pass out for sure.

"Stand your ground!" yelled my companion, moving to my side and trying to insert herself between Richard and me. I clutched at her outstretched arm, but when a shadow fell over us, I looked up to see the man standing again, towering unnaturally tall over Janus.

God...where was my gun then?

I noticed that Richard's collar was undone, and around his neck hung a thick ribbon from which dangled a medallion of a sort. I could not make out what it was.

"Stand ye back, oh shade," ordered my companion. She dipped her free hand into her coat pocket.

The man's mouth twisted around and around, as if attempting to form words but not finding the breath to feed them. For all the world it seemed as if he were struggling with himself.

Suddenly, he lashed out with one hand and struck my companion a mighty blow. It sounded like a gunshot in that small room and it propelled Janus back across the bed. She landed on the other side with a nasty, meaty sound of impact.

Fully alarmed, I waited for the blow that was surely to come for me.

"No," said Richard to me in a voice that was surely not his own, "no, this one here's the problem, not you. Not you *yet*."

With alien speed, he was around the foot of the bed and picking Janus up off the floor with rough attention. I heard her moan, still dazed from the violent blow she took.

"Possession..." she muttered, and Richard shook her like a ragdoll.

I screamed for the man to stop, to try and get him to concentrate on me, but he'd have none of it. He was focused squarely on Janus.

"You're light as a feather, man," he croaked at her. Then his eyes lit up and with one hand he groped at her body.

Richard shook his head, smiled wickedly. "No, not a man at all. A girlie playing at being a man."

He paused, clearly relishing the moment.

"And we have that man you play at. Yes, *we have your man!*"

I surged, finding some energy still within me and channeling it into a desperate move to save the woman...well, never mind that. I moved, and the bastard clocked me so hard my teeth rattled.

Janus tried to speak, but he cuffed her several times with the back of his hand. Turning to me, he swept me off the bed with one quick gesture and I hit the floor, hard, my leg screaming at me in intense pain.

I believe I did lose consciousness for a moment, for when I was able to open my eyes and look up again, the man had my companion pinned to the bed, her shirt torn open and him with his trousers already loosened.

Incredibly, Richard was singing, some low, vulgar ditty that I could barely make out, but so entirely unlike the man we'd been introduced to as Dorothy St. George's salesman of a husband.

He wasn't right at all. He was someone else.

Janus struggled like a wild woman, barely able to speak through the horror and revulsion that most obviously gripped her. I screamed out, struggling to sit up, but I was drowned out by the thunder that boomed outside, shaking the little cabin.

The man's trousers finally loosened and he reached out to repeat the act on my companion. Spittle dripped from his lips as he smacked them together like a starving man over a banquet.

I sat up. Upon the bed, next to Janus, lay an object. My eyes went to it automatically.

The disk.

I reached for it. Everything was soaked with rain; everything. I slipped, my arm sliding off the bedclothes. I lurched forward again, praying I was beyond notice.

Lightning flashed as my fingers closed around the disc.

My brain screamed at me not to look at its face. One side was smooth, the other textured. I felt certain as to which side was which.

With the pain in my leg beyond human ken, I threw myself over Janus and slammed the disk into Richard's leering, lascivious face.

One hand clawed at my arm, but his eyes focused on the disk and he halted all movement. Every muscle in his body tightened and his entire frame became frozen.

"Joshua, let me."

Numbly, I released the disk to Janus. Her smooth, cool fingers closed over mine and reclaimed her property. I fell onto the floor, gazing up at the strange scene before me.

"Spirit," she called out, "be gone from this man! I break your ties to this world, now and forever more. God only knows where you will end."

Richard remained frozen like a statue, the glow behind his eyes now extinguished. My companion struggled a bit to get out from under him, still holding the disk in front of his gaze.

She sighed heavily and shook her head. The torment that arced through her was plainly evident.

"What?" I inquired. "Isn't it—isn't it *gone?*"

"Joshua, oh, Joshua…" she whispered more to herself than me. "Yes, the spirit has departed."

"Then what?"

She turned her face to me; it was ashen.

"This man is also now gone," she said soberly. "No one among the living may look at the face of the artifact. Richard St. George is no more."

All I wanted then was a modicum of peace, a moment to collect myself and *breathe.*

We were to be afforded none of that.

The sound of drums sounded off in the distance, faint but recognizable. I looked up to see Janus hovering over me, her eyes traveling over my limbs, my face.

"Are you all right?" she asked.

I sketched a smile onto my face. "In actuality…no. I am not all right. I am in pain like I've never been in pain ever before. I'm quite certain I shall never walk again."

She knew I wasn't joking; I could see it in her face. Together, we decided it was best to leave me on the floor, with a few pillows beneath my head and a blanket around my legs.

Janus eased Richard off the bed and into a chair. There he sat, staring off into nothingness, his mouth hanging open in a rictus. I felt responsible for his state.

My companion moved over to the window and looked out into the fields.

"Are they out there?"

She nodded in the affirmative. Her stance was that of a military commander, which unnerved me all the more.

"Richard St. George is a casualty of war," she explained in a monotone. "You must realize and accept that, Joshua. We will be overrun here in a matter of minutes, and I must be able to focus on the battle ahead."

I blinked, confused. "Forgive me, my dear, but how do my feelings for *that man* figure into what you do or do not do?"

In a wink she was over me once again, squatting down at my side with her arms folded in front of her, tightly. Her eyes searched through mine, hunting.

"Because you are my strength, my friend. Since the moment I met you, you have been my strength. And I need every bit of it right now."

"Get me over to that goddamned window before you go," I told her, shaking. She started to protest but I silenced her by grasping her hand in mine.

"If I'm going to be your goddamned strength, I need to *see* you."

My companion nodded and, somehow, we got me over to the window without my lapsing into unconsciousness. Propped up against the bed, I surveyed the battlefield and pronounced it good.

She then made to leave.

"Lady Janus," I called after her as she walked over to the door. The old jibe hit her as I intended, and, after a second or two of agitation, she looked over her shoulder at me with what could be classified as a smile.

"Well-played, Joshua. Well-played."

In a moment, I saw her heading away from the cabin and out onto the lawn of tall grass that bordered the fields. The dark clouds rolled and roiled above us, apparently angry at her pluck and courage. The skies darkened and the rain fell heavily once more.

Janus walked to the edge of the field and surveyed the scene. From my vantage point, I could have sworn she was a man, so sure and strong she looked. I chuckled, despite the gloomy situation; she cut a dashing figure.

Far off, lightning illuminated the fields. Figures appeared there and the sound of the drumming, now clearly martial, became clearer.

I looked over at Richard, but he had no interest in the coming battle.

The far-off figures glowed with the same sickly green hue as that of the specter I saw while on the tower. I wondered if perhaps it was that same spirit that had taken up residence in Richard.

Suddenly, I heard the distinct sound of gunfire. Alarmed, I watched as thin streaks of greenish light flew across the fields and toward Janus.

The aim was poor, for the ghostly bullets did not come near my companion.

I blinked away tears to see the next shots came closer; they were finding their range and tightening their aim. My companion did not stir.

I let out with a loud, involuntary gasp when next I saw that the ghostly regiment was abruptly nearer the cabin than I realized. I wiped the wetness from my eyes and leaned closer to the shattered window.

My companion began to move, heading out into the field to engage her opponents. I willed all my remaining strength into her, praying it would do some good. Before her marched two columns of spirits who appeared as soldiers. There was even a flag carried among them.

Shots rang out again and the streaks of light that followed nipped at the edges of Janus' clothes. I yelled out, wishing to the dear Lord I could be out here with her.

My companion plunged into the soldiers' midst. They did not react as living humans would, but their forms wavered as if under water and a large rock had been plunged into the middle of them.

Janus bellowed something and whirled around to swing and swipe her arms through the shades. I blinked and the entire fracas was suddenly only yards away from the cabin, where the fields met the tall grass lawn.

I could see then that the soldiers looked to be of different eras. I recognized uniforms from a hundred years before, but also ones that were only twenty years out of date; there were even a few of current standing. The men's faces were those of corpses and their eyes were white as coddled eggs.

Janus waved her disk at them, centering on one spirit after another. When the face of the artifact appeared before their eyes, they gaped like idiots. Some seemed to melt away, while other more violently disappeared in an expulsion of light and fury.

Perhaps some of the spirits were more resistant to being broken than others, I mused.

Ghostly bayonets came at Janus. These she sidestepped with a yell, but one got through and pierced her side. She grimaced in real pain, but dispensed with her attacker and reached down to snatch up the regiment's flag that had fallen. She held it aloft and yelled out in triumph.

Holding that flag above her head, her coat in tatters and her shirt in disrepair from the rough treatment that Richard had given it, she suddenly reminded me of Delacroix's famous painting of the bare-breasted Liberty leading her people against tyranny.

My lady's actions were magnificent.

One by one, she broke the spirit soldiers' bounds with our mortal coil until I thought she had conquered them all. But I saw that one specter had lagged behind. With rifle in hand, affixed with bayonet, it approached my companion warily.

She paused, looking over at her final enemy. The spirit paused, too. They faced one another in deadly silence.

I was amazed because I thought my eyes were deceiving me: the two figures looked alike.

"We have your man," That's what Richard – or the spirit that had allegedly possessed him – had said during his altercation with Janus.

I had momentarily forgotten that utterance, but it came back to me in full force when I saw my companion facing a soldier that to all appearances could have been her twin brother.

The man was handsome, despite being, of course, *dead*, and somehow missing his cap, I could see that his hair had once been a close-cropped sandy blonde. His features mirrored Janus'. This astounded me.

A bit of something niggled the back of my brain, tried to gain my full attention. I couldn't focus, so intent was I on the battle and lending my thoughts to my companion. Something was trying to tell me something *important*.

I watched as Janus raised her disk and prepared to send her ghostly doppelganger on its way.

I screamed at her to stop. I was certain that we were on the verge of discovering a truth, or on the edge of a great chasm that yawned wide below us.

If she heard me, she didn't heed my warning. The disk came up, the specter *smiled* and looked upon its face.

Then it was gone.

Janus walked off the battlefield empty-handed. After she had secured her disk in her coat pocket, no signs of her opponents or their flag remained to tell the tale. Perhaps, after all that, it was only a metaphorical struggle.

Consciousness eluded me again, I believe; the details are still fuzzy. One moment the rain had stopped and my companion disappeared from my view, the next I opened my eyes to see Dorothy St. George on her knees before her insensate husband, holding him and crying, rocking back and forth.

Strange hands reached out to touch my leg, but gently. An older man I guessed to be the doctor glanced over at me with a quick look and then back to my leg.

"Will it hurt much?" I asked him.

The doctor looked up at Janus, who I realized was now standing next to me, her hand resting on top of my head, and then back to me.

"Yes," he admitted, "most likely quite a bit."

He set my leg. I screamed like a banshee. I passed out again. I will never climb another tower ever again, if ever given the opportunity.

The doctor gave me a fifty-fifty chance of being able to walk without a cane or some other means of support. He left shaking his head and muttering to himself.

Together, my companion and I tried to explain to Dorothy what had happened. I feel certain that she believes us, though their might be some doubt still left in her mind. Though she claimed she understood that Richard will never be the same again, I think she intends to prove us wrong on that score.

After remaining at the cabin for another day, we finally packed up to leave. As we shuffled me into the Lincoln, I asked Janus who was to drive, now that I was something of an invalid.

To my surprise and confusion, she announced that *she* would do the driving from then on.

I promised Dorothy that I would contact her soon and she kissed me on the cheek in thanks. For my companion, she only offered her hand.

As we drove away, I asked if the ghosts would ever return to the property.

"One can never be entirely certain of these things," came the reply, "but I intend to take the fight to its source and *make* certain of it."

"Where are we headed?" I inquired when I saw that we were not pointed toward Janus House. "What are you up to now?"

She reached into a pocket and removed an object. This she tossed over to me as she navigated a curve in the road.

It was the medallion Richard wore about his neck.

"I found another of these, out in the field," she noted, "after I broke those spirits."

Peering at the inscription on the medallion I made out the words there and read them aloud.

"The Order of the Blood-Red Rose."

Janus set her jaw and looked at me out of the corners of her eyes. "We're going beyond those fields, Joshua, to see what lies on the other side."

"To the source of those soldiers," I stated plainly, catching a glimpse of it all.

"Yes," she said. "To the heart of the matter. Are you with me?"

I considered that, but only for a heartbeat.

"Why, we make such a winning team," I announced grimly, "how could it be any other way?"

We drove on.

Chapter VI
DEUS LAPIDEM

"'Fort Temper'," I read out loud to her, lowering the binoculars. She said not a word in reply; it was getting to be quite a habit with us.

I had found the binoculars in a trunk lashed to the back of the Lincoln. With them were another pistol and a collection of items that I can only surmise would be somehow helpful in the investigation of spirits. Chalk, candles, string, a mirror – that sort of thing.

After some driving, Janus and I had come across a military base, there, out in the middle of nowhere. Between the base and the St. Georges' farmstead stretched many miles of open fields.

I asked my companion what we were to do. She remained silent, staring contemplatively at the base. Then, she deigned to speak to me.

"The spirit energies surrounding and permeating this place are appalling and obscene in their magnitude. We must get inside."

It had been three whole days since we came upon Fort Temper. Stymied by the sight of its high fences and its gigantic, ancient-looking stone arch which served as its main gate, we began to drive around, meandering without a plan. It was then that we discovered the little village of Thunstone.

There, we made camp at a small inn and Janus began to scheme her schemes and connive our way onto the base. I, of course, as is my usual state, had no idea *why* we must do such a thing, save that it seemed to be the source of the specters that had bedeviled the poor, unfortunate St. Georges for more than a year.

Thunstone was as good a place as any to rest and recuperate from our ordeal at the farm, especially so for my leg. In fact, and I realize that you may ascribe insanity to my long list of character traits when I admit it, but my leg healed at an abnormal and highly-accelerated rate while in that village.

I believe it had something to do with being in close proximity to my companion.

The first day at the inn, I felt a queer tingling in my leg which I attributed to its break. On the second day I could swear I felt the bone actually knitting itself back together. It was all I could do to not tear the dressings and the brace from it and see what I could see. By the third day I could walk passably well with the use of a silver-headed cane I purchased from a rather pretty young thing in a small antique shop around the corner from the inn.

Janus had no explanation for it. I offered that perhaps some of the medical ability she had seemingly lost was still hanging about her, albeit invisibly, but that brought only a scowl so I dropped that line of investigation.

We drove out to the base late in the afternoon of the third day and scouted our target.

As she said, we needed to somehow get inside it.

Sitting in the automobile once more, she asked me how my leg felt. Warmed by her apparent concern, I informed her that I'd be dancing polkas, schottisches, and waltzes in no time.

"You must be much more careful in the future, Joshua," she said sternly. "You approach angry spirits too blithely – and you have paid the price for it." One long finger indicated my leg.

Since she seemed to be in a chatty mood, I voiced a subject on which I had many questions.

"Why are all these ghosts so *angry* all the time? One would hope the afterlife to be conducive to happiness, or at least complacency…"

Those strange, metallic eyes met mine. "That's just it, Joshua; the spirits we encounter have *not* gone onto what you refer to as an 'afterlife.' The angry ones have carried with him the troubles and travails of their mortal existence, the bitter seed of indignation that we see manifest itself and vex us here, among the living. We do not know exactly why such strong emotion carries over after death – I would agree that it seems strange for it to do so."

She paused, then gave a slight smile. "And they are not *all* so angry, are they?"

"This place," I indicated Fort Temper, "you say it's the source of the soldiers you, err, broke at the farm?"

She nodded. "Yes, I believe so. And I've arrived upon a plan to make entrance."

I settled back into my seat. "Well, I don't suppose we can just—"

Janus threw the Lincoln into gear and sped off toward the base's gate.

"—drive up and ask," I finished, clutching at something to hold onto.

We drove up to the gate and asked. How silly of me to not have thought of it myself.

Of course, our request was refused. The very nice clutch of uniformed men at the gate – all of whom carried rifles, I might add – were very professional in their steadfast assurance that we would not be admitted to the base.

I could feel my companion's frustration rise, spike, and then recede, all in the space of fifteen seconds or so. I half-considered mentioning a great-uncle of mine who had risen to the rank of major in his career when a new and towering figure arrived on the scene.

The soldiers snapped to attention, saluted, and allowed the man to step up to our motorcar.

"This is a private military base," he announced in a clear voice. "How may I help you…?"

He was tall, dark, and good-looking, as these things go. One of those square-jawed, handsome types, just the sort that might find their way into motion pictures after being discovered by a producer with a need for a new leading man. If my reading of his rank was correct, he was a lieutenant. The men around us eyed him warily.

The officer got one good look at my companion and stopped talking.

His mouth moved, forming the shapes for words without also forming an audible component. I'm not all that bad at reading lips, one of the quirks one picks up as a layabout.

118

The man said, "Good Lord."

It wasn't to be the only cause for the man to be startled; his eyes flicked to the seat between Janus and myself whereupon lay the medallion we'd recovered from the fields at the St. Georges' farm. On it was inscribed the symbol of the Order of the Blood-Red Rose.

The officer met my eyes with his, then turned to the soldiers and ordered them to let us through the gates.

On the other side of the massive stone arch, which looked even more ancient the closer I was to it, the man directed us to park the Lincoln off to one side. We did so and exited the vehicle. I quickly pocketed the medallion right before I closed the door.

Our host introduced himself crisply as Lieutenant Ardley Muir. As I complimented myself on accurately deciphering his rank, I noticed my companion's brow lift slightly at his name.

"And you are...?" Muir asked her.

"Janus," she replied and offered her hand in the fashion of one male to another. Our new friend took it after a moment's hesitation.

"Astounding," he remarked, his eyes never leaving her face. "You...you remind me so much of someone I knew....someone *also* named Janus."

"Sgt. *Roman* Janus?" I suggested, stepping forward to offer my own hand. "Joshua Hargreaves, chronicler. Good to know you."

I could see the man was torn by what he was both hearing and seeing. I sympathized with him but stopped short of welcoming him to my world. Instead, I asked the lieutenant how he knew Sgt. Janus.

Muir looked at me, finally, as if I had just dropped in from out of the sky.

"He was my friend, Mr. Hargreaves. We were stationed together here at Temper, several years ago."

Before I could ask him to tell us more, he turned back to my companion. "You are...related to Roman?"

She responded with the same stony silence she often afforded me. I almost felt jealous.

"Don't suppose there's any harm in giving you a quick tour," Muir told us as we began to walk. "We're at a quiet time now. Most of the recent recruits have moved off onto their new assignments."

"You're a training base, then?" I asked, looking around at the scarce buildings, at their plain, blocky shapes and featureless roofs. It was all somewhat depressing.

The lieutenant nodded. "Yes, have been for the last few decades. Was trained myself here, and then asked to be transferred back a few years ago. Couldn't quite, ah, get it out of my system, you know."

I didn't know and couldn't fathom it. I have the utmost respect for those called to serve their country, but I could never, ever wear the uniform myself. Too much marching and shouting and fighting.

"And what do *you* do, err, Miss Janus?" Muir asked my companion, his eyes glancing at me briefly as he inquired.

"Oh, we take care of ghosts," I answered for her in a bored, matter-of-fact manner. "There's a good living in it, you know."

The lieutenant came to a dead stop. I looked up to see that all the color had drained from his face.

He turned to address Janus again. "Maybe…maybe you can *help* with something."

"That's exactly what we are here to do," said she. "Help."

Then she excused herself to walk off a few yards and stand with her arms crossed over her chest and surveying the camp.

It reminded me of that moment back in Canal Chichester when she looked so much to me like a military man, standing there in my coat next to that well. I'll be damned if she didn't look completely at home at Fort Temper.

"Look here, sir," whispered Muir to me. "What's this all about? Is she or is she not related somehow to Roman Janus?"

He made me feel like a school child passing secret notes, but I soldiered on, pouncing on the opportunity.

"I'm afraid I couldn't really say – not with any certainty. I've spent a very, very strange past few months with this woman and still know next to nothing about her. Tell me, lieutenant; if you were to imagine her with long black hair and wearing a midnight-blue frock, would you then say she was familiar to you?"

He considered that for a moment, but shook his head. "No, no not at all. She only reminds me of Roman. Good old Roman – what an odd bird he was."

"Tell me, *please*," I said, not wanting to sound overly desperate.

"Like I said, we were stationed here together," Muir told me, "two young bucks with all the gumption to take on the world. Roman was from good stock, much better'n me, but he wanted in on the lowest rung, not take the 'easy way' up the ladder by coming in as an officer out of the academy. He wanted to come in as an enlisted man and get his hands dirty.

"And he did. Swiftest rise to the rank of sergeant ever seen here, they said. Roman was a soldier's soldier, all spit and polish, but not afraid to get down in the mud and help a friend to his feet. Not like my brother, who was here with us, too."

The lieutenant paused there, eyes blinking, remembering something from another time.

"Janus, ah, obviously didn't stay here then," I interjected. "From what I understand, he operated more recently in the private sector."

"Lost track of him," Muir replied solemnly. "After he…after he was forcibly discharged."

I was stunned. I admit it. That was the last thing I expected to hear. It made my poor leg ache, or so I imagined.

Before I could say much more or ask another question, "Miss Janus" started to stalk back toward us.

"I should like to know more about that, lieutenant," I whispered out of the side of my mouth, in what I hoped was a kindly, friendly way.

"Not much more I *can* tell you, Mr. Hargreaves," Muir said, "but there's a file here at the base on Roman Janus. I know more of the situation, but I'm duty-bound to not repeat it, you know."

"And this?" I slipped the medallion from my pocket and showed it to him, centered in the palm of my hand. The lieutenant gave it a quick, almost cursory glance, then straightened again when Janus walked back up to us.

Wondering how in hell I could get my hands on that file, I bit down on my tongue and forced a wan smile on my face for my companion.

"Have a good think?" I asked her.

Her eyes were fairly sparking and I shrunk back a bit from them.

"The occult power that occupies this place is staggering," she announced. "We must get to work immediately."

Lieutenant Muir apparently took that pronouncement mostly in stride, for he only dipped his chin and with a wave of his hand urged us to walk with him again.

"The camp itself," he said, cutting off any questions from us, "is roughly sixty years old, maybe a bit more. As you may have guessed from the look of the stone arch at the gates, there's been activity here for far longer."

I guessed that his little history speech was to divert his thoughts from something else, something that pressed down on him. Muir seemed nervous and I wondered if we might be thrown out of Fort Temper at any moment.

"That larger building there," said Janus, pointing at a long, low structure that sat in the center of the camp. "What is it? Can we go there?"

Muir looked around us, his eyes shifting back and forth, side to side. He licked his lips.

"Yes," he said, quietly, "but not now. Later. I can take you there later. For now, I'll need to take you back to your automobile."

Before we knew what was happening, the lieutenant marched us back to the Lincoln, told us to get in, and then said he'd return in an hour or so. My companion quite clearly was not in favor of the idea, but she clamped her mouth shut and took her place behind the wheel. I struggled into my seat, being careful not to jostle my leg, and together we watched the man stride off and round a corner.

As we sat and waited, I debated with myself over whether or not I should tell her what I had learned of Roman Janus. Would it have made a difference to her then if she knew? She seemed focused, which was potentially a good thing. But then again, when she was focused, she also tended to get us into trouble.

I must have sighed out loud, for she asked me what was the matter.

"Though I've sat and watched a number of good years of my youth pass by me back home, I still can't stomach waiting."

"Waiting," she noted, "is a large part of the investigation of spirits. You have laid a solid foundation for a career in my profession, Joshua."

"I find that infinitely comforting," I told her with a straight face. Then, I asked her if she had ever been to the base before.

"Not that I am aware. It does seem very...familiar to me, though. As if someone had described it to me at some point in time."

I sat up and leaned a little in her direction. "Who?" I asked. "Can you think on that a moment? *Who* would have told you about it? Only soldiers come here – besides us, of course."

She did not turn her head to me. She sat there and stared out past the windshield. After a moment, her eyelids began to flutter and her chest rose and sank in a somewhat hurried fashion. Suddenly, she dipped her chin to her breastbone and then raised it up again.

"In a letter," Janus said in a voice that was not exactly hers, yet it was. "He writes me many letters. He gets awfully lonely at times. He doesn't care much for his commander..."

Scarcely being able to believe my ears, I pushed on.

"*Who* has written you these letters, my dear?"

Her eyelids fluttered again and a small smile played across her lips. "My...love."

Further inquiries could not flush out a name and I gave it all up after a minute or so, worried that she might come out of the strange state in fiery anger at my presumption.

We sat there for the rest of our wait in silence.

Lieutenant Muir returned to us as the sun began to set, bringing a more tangible gloom to the already-murky surroundings. We then marched over to the building we'd spied earlier and that had drawn my companion's attention.

Closer to the structure, I could see that it appeared a bit older then the others around it, and without windows. Curious, I hastened to Muir's side as he held the door for Janus and invited us inside.

We entered into a darkened room. The lieutenant shut the door behind us and threw a latch on it. I fingered the pistol in my coat pocket.

When the lights were raised I saw we were in a kind of meeting hall. Rows upon rows of benches led to a podium at the front of the area, and hanging on the surrounding walls were a score of framed paintings. In between each painting sat a stand holding a flag on a pole.

Janus was silent as she began to walk through the room. I noticed that she seemed to have little interest in the room's décor, but glanced back and forth between the ceiling and the floor. I'd almost have sworn that she was sniffing around like a hunting dog.

Seeing as how our host was also holding his tongue, I walked over to the nearest painting and saw that it was simply a staid representation of Fort Temper itself. The next one showed a battle from roughly a hundred years ago. As I walked along, I found more battles depicted, and I surmised that they boasted of the participation of the camp's recruits over the years.

Finding myself at the front of the room, I looked up at the very large work that hung behind the podium: a military man of great presence, with short-cropped silver hair, a good-sized moustache and cold steel eyes. His mouth, what could be seen below the moustache, was unsmiling.

I hesitated to approach the painting, but stepped up to it to read the small plate affixed to it at the bottom.

Upon reading the plate, I called out to my companion.

Janus was at my side in an instant, perhaps sensing my dismay. I bid her to read what I had read on the plate. The dates there ended some ten years hence, indicating the man's demise.

"Major-General Willis Frank Havelock" intoned my companion, straightening up again to catch my eye.

"Yes," I nodded. "No doubt in my mind. A relation of Valerie's. Look at the eyes."

It was plain to see that she agreed with me; I was glad that I didn't need to debate the issue for I could find no words after the revelation. The feeling that the universe was a much, much smaller place than I had previously imagined had stunned me into mute contemplation.

"This is what I wanted you to see."

We spun around to look at Muir, who had come up quietly behind us and spoken in a voice from beyond the grave.

I looked back to the painting. It was of the typical variety of military portraits, with a sparse background and overall dark atmosphere. The technique was good; Havelock looked quite realistic. Then, among the many medals that sprouted from his chest like a bouquet of metal flowers, I spotted a familiar symbol. A small medallion of bronze.

The Order of the Blood-Red Rose.

"I see it, Joshua." She'd noticed my gaze, obviously, and stilled my hand as I reached into my pocket to retrieve the medallion there.

"This man holds a place of some importance at this facility," she told Muir, "but that's not what you wanted us to see. He's still here, isn't he?"

The lieutenant gulped. Suddenly, he appeared quite nervous, as if a small boy who'd been caught doing something he shouldn't. I watched as his eyes scanned the painting then glanced around the room.

"Yes," he admitted in a quiet tone. "Yes, I brought you here because…because the major-general needs to be put to rest. When you said that you…you *took care of ghos*ts, I thought…"

"No one else need know that we are here," my companion assured him. "Here to break this spirit and allow him the reward I am sure he deserves. I have questions, but for now the only one that really matters is…can we be left alone to work?"

Muir's eyes went wide as he gazed again at the Havelock's portrait. "He was a cruel man in life, ruled this camp with a steel fist. By the book, always by the book, and when that wasn't enough, wrote his own rules."

Running a hand through his hair, he gulped again. "Some of the men loved him. The rest, well…they wished him dead, to be honest. He was funny like that, inspiring one moment, torturous the next. You could never fully *trust* him, for if you did, he'd turn on you like a snake and his punishments were severe…"

"Go now," ordered Janus, gesturing with one hand toward the door. "You've been very helpful, lieutenant – now I will return the favor."

Muir squared his shoulders, trying to reclaim a bit of dignity, no doubt. I pitied him then, knowing that for a man like himself, an admittance of weakness was like being shot.

At the door, he turned to us. "Havelock had a few very special adversaries on a very short list. Roman Janus was one of those."

Exiting, the lieutenant shut the door behind him, leaving us in the great hall alone and with our thoughts.

I started babbling.

"I'm trying to piece this all together," I informed her, "to make sense of it, if any sense *can* be made of it. God knows nothing else has over the past few months."

I looked up at Havelock's dour features, his frozen eyes. "Muir wants us to get rid of this spirit – he's an awfully trusting soul, isn't he? I mean, letting us loose on a military base – civilians! I don't like it. And this major-general...its Valerie's father, right? Who else could it be, according to those dates? And he and Sgt. Janus were enemies of some sort, maybe because of her."

I paused, glimpsing something just out of reach.

"Valerie said that she knew Janus, and we had that confirmed by the newspaper accounts we read. She also said she reacted strongly when she learned that *you* also hunted ghosts...but she claimed that you were a 'charlatan' just like the man himself."

The major-general frowned down at me. I rushed ahead.

"What if," I said, "what if Valerie and Janus were...romantically involved and—"

My companion rounded on me suddenly, eyes ablaze.

"Joshua, *shut up.*"

Surprised at first, I realized what I had been doing and quieted myself. She turned her back to me and began to pace up and down one aisle between the benches.

"Let *me* think, will you?" she seethed. "Yes, Havelock is most definitely Valerie's father and there must obviously be a thread of stubborn practicality that runs through them both. But that doesn't concern me at the moment."

She turned to look at me. "Muir knows of the Order of the Blood-Red Rose; that's obvious, too. Havelock was most likely the leader of it and the farm figures into that, most likely one of their meeting places some years ago. But, the Order's roots are *here*, and they are twisted and dark."

Reaching out one hand, she gripped a bench and wobbled at the knees. I sprang over to her to steady her, but she waved me off with a curt slash of her other hand.

"The spirit energies here are monstrous, as I have already told you. This building must sit on top of one of the largest concentrations I've ever…" She paused, her eyes losing focus. Then, she asked me to hand her the medallion.

I pulled it out of my pocket and was about to relinquish it to her when I saw something move on the far end of the hall, off in the shadows there.

A man.

I completed the transference of the medallion to Janus and together we walked toward the man. Well, *I* hobbled, but you get the point.

As we drew nearer to the figure, I could see that he was very old, most likely in his eighties. Dressed in a grey smock of some sort, he seemed to me like a wizened old friar, or a country parson fallen on hard times.

Janus stopped some fifteen or so feet from the man and held up the medallion for him to see. His eyes went from its face to hers and then glanced fleetingly at mine. It was only a split second that his gaze lingered on me, but for that moment I felt clammy all over.

"May we pass?" my companion inquired. The little figure said nothing, only raised his hairy eyebrows in question.

"Seems to want something more," I offered, but Janus hissed at me to be quiet.

"No, not that," she whispered then. I wasn't certain what she meant. Another sign? Hopefully not blood or some other idiotic offering, I thought to myself.

The man's eyebrows went up again in question, then fell back down again and wrung themselves in confusion. Janus, in growing exasperation, asked him what else it was he wanted.

Closing his eyes and wagging his round little head from side to side, the man stepped back into the shadows, melting away from our sight.

My companion crumpled to the floor.

Though it pained my leg immensely, I struggled to get her up off the floor and onto one of the benches. Sitting next to her and propping her up, I chuckled mirthlessly. My leg was aching something fierce, though it had not done so previously while in her presence.

"Where am I?"

My companion's question startled me, even frightened me a bit. I hugged her to me, instinctively, though I almost immediately regretted such a reaction – but she seemed so *lost* at the moment.

"You wouldn't believe me if I told you," I whispered in her ear as I gazed around at our present location.

Suddenly feeling very bold, I pulled back from the embrace to look at her face. "Who are you?" I asked, carefully and slowly.

She placed two fingers very tentatively on my lips, searching my face with her beautiful eyes, now with a strange, warm cast that I had never seen before in them.

"I am…I am…"

The far door to the hall opened. I pulled my lady off the bench and to the floor, clamping a hand over her mouth. My leg screamed at me in protest. I scooted us under the bench and held her tightly to me, silently transmitting my very great wish that she would remain silent.

Many people filtered into the hall. One after another, with the sound of their boots echoing around the walls and ceiling. Down on the floor, it was almost deafening. But, then, only a short distance into the room, the sound of their footfalls faded off and the figures seemed to glide into the area like…spirits.

A hand touched mine, the one I had pressed over her mouth, signaling that she would be fine on her own recognizance. It took me only one quick glance at her face to see that Janus had returned.

The procession of men moved down the center aisle of the hall in a double line toward our position. Even from under the bench I could feel their military bearing, though every one of them wore a dark red cloak that rustled ever so softly as they walked. I took a chance and peered up and over the bench. I saw then that the men each sported a voluminous hood that obscured his head and face.

"The Order," whispered Janus. I nodded in agreement.

One figure, in the middle of the line, wore no hood. He was a young man, his hair cropped so short as to almost be non-existent. His eyes darted back and forth with a nervous twitch, but he kept moving along with the others.

To say it was all a strange sight would be an understatement. There was a religious atmosphere about it, yet also a profanity that defied words. I wanted to yell at the figures, scare them off. They ought not to be convened so – it was an overwhelming sense of wrongness that came over me as I watched them.

One by one they passed by the podium at the front of the room and turned their heads to look up at the portrait of Major-General Havelock. The eyes in the painting did not move, but I would have sworn in a court of law that they looked down on the procession and found it satisfactory. I for one could barely tear my own gaze from it all.

Finally, the line arrived upon the spot where we had seen the little old man. From out of the shadows he appeared once more and the first figure in line reached into his robes and produced a medallion on a cord. The old man's eyebrows lifted and the hooded figure said something.

The old man allowed him to pass. The scenario was repeated for each cloaked man.

I could not hear what each of them said, but every time they spoke, the walls of the great room shuddered and vibrated.

Janus gave a curt nod of her chin and we crept closer, crawling along the floor and toward the procession.

When the young man who wore no hood approached the small, wizened figure, the man next to him stepped forward and, with one arm around the shoulders of the aspirant, he produced his medallion and spoke a single word:

"*Stenndec.*"

The young man flinched violently. His patron – for lack of a better term – held onto him and steered him past the old man. Apparently, the hooded figure spoke for them both.

Without realizing that I had turned my head to her, I found myself looking into Janus' eyes and with my mouth agape. Her strange orbs were watery, but the look on her face told me that she had heard the word too and that a piece of the puzzle had been shifted into place.

Moments later, we stood in the great hall by ourselves again, with only the disapproving features of Major-General Havelock for company.

"Sickening," she spat out, walking slowly toward the darkened corner of the hall where the procession had been. "Come, Joshua."

"Where?"

"After them, of course."

She stepped back over to the podium and sized up a short piece of cloth that hung from its front. On it was embroidered the official seal of Fort Temper. With one swift movement, she ripped it away and walked over to me.

"I shall wear the hood and speak the word," she informed me matter-of-factly, placing the cloth over her head to form a makeshift hood. "You will be the new recruit."

I had no strength to argue with her. Gripping my cane, I positioned myself in the proper place and Janus stepped beside me and put her arm around my shoulders.

The old man materialized from the shadows. My companion raised the medallion of the Order of the Blood-Red Rose; he raised his eyebrows.

"*Stenndec*," she hissed, as if the word would burn her tongue if she gave it even the slightest of volume and strength.

It hit *me* like a freight train. I spasmed from its punch, staggered. Janus held onto me, somehow.

We were allowed to pass.

Had we gone through a door? A portal of some kind? I wish I could say with certainty, but I was still reeling from that word when I looked up to see we stood on a kind of landing with a canopy of heavy wooden beams and supports over our heads. The wood looked very old, but solid, I supposed.

"God-Tongue," she said.

Dizzy, I eyed her cautiously. "Come again?"

Janus slid her arm from my shoulders and stepped over to the edge of the landing. Together we looked down upon a set of stairs that descended into the earth…into inky darkness.

"The language of the Divine," she pronounced. "Once having spoken it, I understand. The word is of the God-Tongue, the alleged holy speech of the Almighty."

I protested vehemently. How was it that in such places of malaise as the St. George's farmhouse and the camp a "divine" word could be spoken? And even if there was such a thing as a "God-tongue," how would we mere mortals even know of it, let alone be able to speak it?

"Something is allowing it," explained Janus. "Something has opened the passage between this plane and the next and let divine knowledge pass through it. It's utterly blasphemous."

My own tongue simply sputtered and fell short on any rational rebuttal. I could only agree with her that it was entirely *wrong*, though I was too inexperienced in matters of faith and the philosophy behind it to formulate further coherent thoughts on it. It quite literally boggled my mind.

Had I only known what lay ahead I might have chided myself for believing the most unbelievable was behind us.

"Never speak that word," Janus cautioned me and began to descend into the darkness.

Several feet down, the stairs turned and began to wind in on themselves. Our eyes began to adjust to the shadows and we could hear voices somewhere below us. What was only a light breeze of air at the landing became a howling wind as we reached the bottom of the stairs and found ourselves in a small chamber of rock and earth. Across from the last step sat a wooden door in the natural wall.

It creaked slightly when we opened it, but the voices we had heard emanated from beyond it, so we pressed forward and prayed we wouldn't be heard. I wondered how far below the surface we were but failed at guessing.

The door opened into a larger chamber, an incredible cave formation lit by myriad candles that sat in small, natural alcoves throughout the open area. Above us, stalactites stretched down from the cave's ceiling like a series of sharp teeth. Water dripped down here and there, giving the chamber a murky, swampy feel.

We stepped over to a low bulwark of earth that formed a kind of break between the immediate area we occupied and the rest of the large chamber. It provided us with a good place to hunker down and observe our new surroundings – and our fellow cave-dwellers.

The procession had spread out to form an audience that separated to two sides and sat down on wooden pews. Candles in tall holders sat at the front of the crowd, creating an orb of greater illumination there. Three hooded figures stood in the globe of light facing their audience. I could see that the young, hoodless man had been placed in the front row. He looked wan and drawn.

One of the three men at the front stepped forward and addressed the hooded figures.

"The three-hundredth-and-sixty-sixth conclave of the Order of the Blood Red Rose will now come to order. We present to you a new branch to extend our reach and to enrich the growth of the body. The Order will be rich with new blood and will never wither and die."

The man raised his hands and spread them wide. "How say you all?" he called out in a loud, booming voice.

A murmur of assent rippled through the audience; there was a definite lack of enthusiasm, or so I gleaned from the tone of their response.

"Let the new branch come forward and take his place at the side of those who came before."

The young man – who now looked even younger – was brought up to the three leaders and left there, wide-eyed and slack-jawed.

"Yes," I whispered to Janus, guessing at her thoughts, "I have my pistol, dammit."

The three hooded figures stepped aside and someone doused the candles in their tall holders. The only light in the chamber then came from the smaller candles that littered the outer walls.

Something beyond the three men glowed softly. Something large that sat low to the ground. Our viewing spot was somewhat raised and we got a good glimpse of it.

A spike of alarm shot through my companion. I felt it even though I was not touching her at that moment. I had never truly seen her frightened before then.

"What?" I implored her. "What is it?"

"*Deus Lapidem*," she sobbed, "the God-Stone…"

Janus was gone. In her place, she left a quivering young lady, tear-streaked and frightened beyond measure.

I forced her to look at me. The atmosphere in the chamber was suddenly thick and charged with a force I could not comprehend. I begged her to tell me what the thing was that we looked upon.

She could only stare at it, mouthing silent words. I wondered if she might be praying.

On the floor of the great cave sat a large stone, some eight feet long by what I would have guessed to be at least three feet wide. The stone was almost flat on top, save for some kind of depressions at its rough center. Overall, it looked to be a natural formation; a huge rock lifted up from the earth and set down in this hideous, underground grotto.

A soft light emanated from within it, pulsing like a heartbeat. My eyes clouded up as I looked at it and I wiped at them with my coat sleeve.

It was tears. I was crying myself.

"No, no, no, no…"

The woman beside me had found her voice again. I held her arms, trying not to shake her, though I wanted to. She saw my tears and stammered out words.

"The God-Stone – the last place on Earth that Our Lord stood. The very spot from where his disciples watched Him depart, from where our long wait for His return began…His footprints may still be seen atop the Stone…"

She believed everything she said; I could see it in her eyes, as her hands ran over her head and hair, seemingly not comprehending that her long, black locks were gone.

"Surely that's in *Jerusalem*," I insisted, "in a *church* there! I've seen pictures of it!"

There was something in what I said – a challenge, perhaps. Her face changed almost immediately, so swiftly that it scared me. Janus was back.

"There are many things in Jerusalem that aren't what they seem to be, Joshua," she said, visibly collecting herself. "Much of it is for tourists – I assure you that *this* is indeed *Deus Lapidem*, though I wish most fervently that it would be anything but.

"It's a conduit of sorts, opened when Christ left our world. Legend has it that it will remain open until He returns. Look there."

I looked. Figures had risen from the Stone.

A new procession had begun. The ghostly shades of men in uniform wafted up from the artifact and were making their way, single-file, down the empty center aisle between the two sides of the audience. The cloaked and hooded figures bowed their heads as they passed.

The God-Stone continued to pulse with its eerie, pale internal illumination, but I got the strong feeling that it did so weakly and with only a bare fraction of its true power.

The spirits of the soldiers were uniformed in trappings of many different eras. I knew for a certainty that what we had witnessed at the farm sprung from this same source. It was all ghastly, an utter perversion of nature; I wanted to shut it all down, so horrible was it in its skewing of life and death.

"Walk with them," commanded one hooded man to the young aspirant. "Now!"

The boy hesitated, then shook his head violently while he mouthed his refusal over and over. Another of the three leaders, shook his own head in resignation, then nodded to the figure next to him.

That one produced a long, wicked-looking knife and stepped toward the boy's back.

"*No!*" I screamed, standing up in outrage.

A sea of hoods whipped around to stare at me. The glint of metal caught my eye and I realized that pistols had been produced from beneath robes. I fumbled for my own.

Shots rang out, booming in the echoing cavern. The bulwark of earth in front of me exploded in many places, bullets chewing it to pieces.

Before I dove to the ground, I spotted the young man crumpling in his place, a knife sticking out of his back.

As I fell, I saw that Janus had stood up as well and was brandishing a pistol – most likely the one I'd found in the trunk from the Lincoln. She held it without conviction, though, and I glanced from her to the crowd of hooded men and spotted one of them draw a bead on her.

I fired without thinking. The man sprung back, as if punched in the chest by an invisible opponent. There was no question in my mind that he was not dead before he hits the ground.

I had killed a man.

Shots exploded all around us, Janus and me. She returned fire immediately, though it took me a moment to echo the sentiment. There was blood on my hands, staining them forever.

Through the haze of the smoke that filled the chamber, I saw that the ghosts of the soldiers had disappeared, gone back to whatever place from which they had come. Good riddance.

"Fire!" bellowed someone, and there was no need to look around to see what was meant. Candles had been disturbed in their holders and had fallen onto one of the wooden pews. The flame from the

135

candles licked out hungrily at the wood and within two blinks of the eye the pew was a blazing pyre.

The hooded men stampeded toward us, seeking the stairs back up to the surface. They fired at us, hoping to clear a path for their hasty exit.

"Let them pass!" yelled Janus from somewhere in the heavy smoke that choked the cavern. I hoped out of the way, allowing my would-be murderers to run past me and to the stairs.

My companion ran toward the God-Stone. I couldn't stop her.

Then I heard her call to me. She'd found something. I crawled on my hands and knees, my leg suddenly feeling almost normal. When I approached her, I saw that she squatted over a prone figure, a man in a cloak and hood. She pulled the hood back to reveal Lieutenant Muir.

He'd been shot. I forced myself to not waste a moment wondering from whose bullet he'd been wounded. Blood leaked from the side of his mouth, so I assumed it was not well off.

"You bastard," I spat at him. "What were you playing at? For God's sake, did you want us all killed?"

Muir smiled. He actually smiled. "No," he coughed, "I…I hoped you'd get rid of our ghosts…been terrible of late, you know."

"Muir!" Janus interjected. "What is the Order? What do they hope to accomplish?"

The man coughed up more blood, but the smile never left his lips.

"They were good once," he slurred. "Good, in the beginning. Roman…was a member…we were caretakers, of…of the Stone. Then, Havelock cocked it all up…got too greedy with the…with the *power*. Roman told him what he could do with it all."

The fire was growing more intense, spreading to the other pews. It was getting very, very difficult to breathe. I tried to lift Muir, but he screeched at me to let him be.

"Done, I'm done," he whispered. "Tried to set it to right, but…but…"

He focused his eyes on my companion.

"Don't-don't let me stay here…please, God…send me on…"

"Who am I?" she demanded of him.

He smiled again. "Janus…"

He died and she broke the tether, whatever it was that held his soul to the Earth.

At the foot of the stairs, I grabbed at her arm. "Will they even let us up? They could just lock us down here until we die."

"No," she assured me, "there's too much at stake for them. They'll wonder what we'd do with the Stone, for one. They'll want answers. Up we go."

The fire most likely would not harm the Stone, I thought, and when they had cleared us out, they could set up shop in the chamber all over again and continue with their obscene rites. The taste of it in my mouth was a putrid thing.

Up we went, though our lungs were wretched from the smoke. Thankfully, my leg felt almost healed.

At the top of the steps, at the far side of the landing, we found a large open doorway, the one we'd obviously come through before but without realizing it. Brandishing my cane and my pistol, I nodded at Janus and we walked through it. Beyond it was another flight of stairs, a short one that ended at another landing and another door.

That door was open and a hooded figure stood there. In his hand he held a pistol.

"We left word with the Thunstone police that we were coming here and that if we did not return that they should seek us out," my companion informed the man. "Can't we talk about this like adults?"

The man turned to someone behind him and conversed briefly with them. Then, he stepped back out of the door way and, waving the pistol, gestured for us to approach.

Just as we were about to walk through the door, Janus raised her firearm for me to see and cocked an eyebrow at me.

"Do it," I urged her.

She fired two shots into one of the large wooden beams that appeared to hold up the ceiling over the spiral staircase. The wood splintered from the bullets and then cracked with a loud explosion of dust and debris.

The whole thing then came a'tumblin' down.

The roar of the collapsing earth and wooden supports drowned out the shouts of our hooded hosts. The chaos that ensued was all-encompassing. Somehow, we slipped past the lot of them – I only had to bean one or two of them with my cane as we ran from the building and across the camp to our automobile.

Janus got the damn thing started and we turned to see the entire great hall collapse in on itself with a great expression of sound and fury.

We drove off into the night, feeling certain that *Deus Lapidem* would never, ever be seen again by human eyes.

"I should think you'll have quite a bit to write about when we get back to the house," she said to me over the whipping wind.

I gave her a small smile and returned to my thoughts. She was correct; there was much to sort through and to chronicle.

"And you?" I asked her after a moment's silence, knowing damn well that she would return to that wretched forbidden room of hers and I wouldn't see her for days. Screwing up my courage to say just that, I bit down on the inclination and simply looked out at the scenery.

"Maybe they didn't really have Sgt. Janus like it said," I suggested. "That…thing that possessed Richard St. George, I mean. Maybe it was lying. I'd like to think that *he* wouldn't get caught up in a business like that…"

Silence, as always. In a way, I began to feel a sense of success when I got her to clam up, like I was hitting close to the truth.

The sun was just starting to come up as we turned onto the little road to Janus House, just outside of Mount Airy. A small collection of automobiles waited for us in front of the house. Among them stood several people.

"If you jump out now, I could grab the wheel and claim I never saw you," I joked. She, of course, commanded me to be quiet.

As we neared the assemblage, I saw that two of the vehicles sported the markings of the Mount Airy Police Department. Another one was a very expensive Cadillac.

I had a very bad feeling about it.

My companion drove up beside the small crowd and stopped.

Killing the engine, she alighted from the Lincoln and faced a smartly-dressed man who stepped over to her with two uniformed policemen in tow.

It was then that I saw Valerie Havelock-Mayer in the back of the Caddy, with dark circles under eyes, looking like she had spent the night sitting in her motorcar.

"Is this her?" the man in the suit inquired of the woman. Valerie pursed her ruby lips and nodded.

"Yes, Captain Mumford – that's her," she intoned in a raspy voice.

The captain turned back to my companion. "Do you answer to the name of 'Janus'?"

"Yes."

"And have you taken up residence in this house?"

"Yes."

"Do you know the whereabouts of its true owner?"

"*I* am its owner," my companion told the man.

"Then," said the police captain, frowning, "it is my duty to inform you, ma'am, that you are now under arrest for the murder of Sgt. Roman Janus."

With that, he nodded to the officers beside him and they placed handcuffs on Janus' wrists. She did not resist, to her credit, though her brow was creased with confusion. I nearly jumped out of my skin at the blatant ridiculousness of it all and told the captain what I thought of it.

"Hold your tongue, lad," he snapped, jabbing a finger into my sternum, "or we'll be hauling you off next."

As the dust from their departing vehicles swirled around me, I reasoned that my life could become no stranger, nor crumble so completely into shambles.

Oh, how wrong I was.

Chapter VII

JUST LIKE JAZZ

It took me four whole days to convince them to let me see her, to let me talk with her.

The Mount Airy jail was a wretched place, a crumbling artifact of a bygone day that was barely fit for human habitation. I fully expected it to still say "gaol" on wooden plank hung haphazardly above the door. No ghosts; what self-respecting spirit would choose to stay there?

Janus looked awful. I found her sitting on the edge of an old cot in a tiny cell, staring at the floor, her skin pallid and her demeanor dark. She barely glanced up to me as I was ushered into the room of cells.

I found it horribly ironic that she who was accused of murder yet was innocent would be behind bars, yet I who had recently killed a man retained my freedom…such as it was.

"You needn't castrate yourself over it, Joshua," she said plainly, apparently reading my mind. I didn't care much for her choice of words and told her so. Janus smiled wanly and looked up at me. Her eyes had been drained of their luster and alien quality. Now, they only looked tired and deflated.

"But how do you mean?" I inquired, pulling up a ramshackle stool from a corner. "That man—"

"Was trying to *kill* me," she seethed. "You protected me. There was no real choice in the situation. You did the right thing. He was a villain and he has paid for his crimes."

She spoke the words with such finality, such conviction that it left no room for argument. I pushed the matter to the back of my brain; it was my own cross to bear and I had other more pressing matters to speak on.

I told my companion that her trial had been set for three days hence but that she had no attorney to represent her. We both agreed that while my services were adequate in Canal Chichester I would hardly be up to snuff to argue a murder case in Mount Airy. Thank goodness they hadn't hauled her off to the city – Mount Airy was the county seat and where the alleged murder had taken place.

"How can they charge you with murder without a body as evidence of such?" I mused aloud.

Janus continued to stare at the dirty floor of her cell and shrugged. "They feel they have no choice, I presume. Madame Havelock-Mayer's word holds much weight in the area – she has obviously convinced the authorities that there is no other explanation for…for…"

She couldn't continue. The words wouldn't come. She simply couldn't separate herself from Roman Janus.

"Joshua," she whispered, looking up at me with great pain etched upon her face, "I don't feel well. I've been too long in…in this place. My mind is…going to pieces."

We sat quietly for several silent minutes.

"It's just like jazz, isn't it?" I offered. Her face told me that she wasn't following my line of reason.

"You take all these discordant bits, all these threads you have lying about, and you make something *more* of them. That's what you've done for *months* now, since the moment I met you. And you'll do it again. You'll see."

She stretched out a hand from between the bars and took one of mine.

"'Just like jazz'," she repeated. "You're a very odd man, Joshua Hargreaves."

I wanted to point out the absurdity of that statement, considering who and where she was, but held my wise counsel. We had plans to make.

Over the seven days between Janus' arrest and the beginning of her trial, the police had made several visits to Janus House. I allowed them in, knowing full well they'd find no evidence of a murder. It was mildly amusing to see them wandering the halls and getting lost; the house seemed very subdued at the time, as if hiding its true nature from the strangers within its walls.

On the day of the trial, I arrived at the Mount Airy courthouse to find Miss Wendy Jackson waiting there for me on its steps. She looked very fetching and I had to remind myself what she had done to Janus and me when we last met.

"I couldn't keep away, Joshua," she said as she took my arm and steered me toward the entrance to the building. I must have stiffened under her overly-familiar gesture, for she scowled and swatted at my shoulder.

"Now, now," Wendy whispered in my ear, "I know you're angry with me, but you need all the friends you can get at the moment. Now tell me why you're walking with a cane..."

My mind wrestled with itself, remembering her betrayal at Christmas Hall, but also the feel of her soft lips on mine. I resolved to let her think I had tabled the matter – perhaps I could gain more insight on Valerie Havelock-Mayer through her.

We found seats near the front of the audience box in the courtroom and settled in. As we chatted a bit about my leg, I noticed that Wendy had very pretty ankles.

Suddenly she was somber and serious. "Why has it come to this, Joshua? Why haven't you looked into Sgt. Janus' disappearance before this?"

What could I tell her? I was too wrapped up in traipsing around on adventures? The thought of it was abruptly and awkwardly absurd, and the words I contrived to speak on it were like ashes in my mouth. Thankfully, court was called to order and we turned away from each other and looked across the courtroom.

The judge – a portly man with wild tufts of hair wafting about his dome of a head – came in, we all rose and then sat again, and then Janus was brought in and it was announced that she would be representing herself. She looked a bit better then she had in her cell; perhaps my words of encouragement had brought her some strength.

Valerie Havelock-Mayer arrived late and was escorted to a spot in the front row, thankfully nowhere near me. I saw her look imperiously around the courtroom and settle her eyes on Wendy and then myself. She then dismissed both of us by taking out a small compact and powdering her nose.

The announcement came that the defendant in the case – given the name "Mary Smith," for she refused to reveal her real name – would be representing herself.

My stomach dropped at that.

The prosecutor issued his opening statement, saying that he'd show that foul play was indeed the crime that had been committed and that he had evidence to back that up. I snorted; the man had no evidence that I knew of.

Continuing, the prosecutor noted that "Sgt. Roman Janus was a prominent citizen of Mount Airy" and his disappearance had caused much "worry and concern." Inwardly, I rankled at that – the townspeople most likely had no real idea the man was not about until Valerie Havelock-Mayer made a fuss.

The man ended his statement and looked to Janus. She in turn shook her head, and in doing so passed on her right to make her own opening remarks. I thought it wise as it seemed to show her utter contempt for the proceedings. But, what do I know?

The trial then continued. The first witness for the prosecution was called: Valerie Havelock-Mayer.

"How do you know Roman Janus, Madame? When did you first meet?"

Valerie did not smile at the prosecutor's question, but got some kind of damn-fool far-off kind of look on her face.

"My father," she began, "the late Major-General Willis Havelock, was stationed as the commandant of Fort Temper when I was a young girl and I lived with him there. My mother had died in childbirth, you see, and my father swore to always have me with him. I met Roman Janus there at the base." Valerie stopped there, as if she wished to stay more but chose to not to.

"And you got to know him well?"

"Yes," answered Valerie. "I saw him rise from the rank of private to sergeant within only a few short years."

"And, please pardon me for the question, but what was the culmination of your relationship with Janus?"

The woman's eyes closed, then opened again. "We were engaged to be married, sir."

"*That's a lie!*"

All heads swiveled to take in the sight of my companion, standing there and pointing one accusing finger at the witness.

"The judge banged his gavel over the audience's hub-bub. "If that constitutes a formal objection, Miss Smith," he chided, "then I shall have to overrule it. Counselor?"

The man gave a short bow of his head. "Thank you, your honor. Now then, Madame Havelock-Mayer, how was it that you and the sergeant were not married?"

Valerie gulped, a gesture I felt was staged. "We...something occurred, something which mystifies me to this day. Roman was dishonorably discharged from the service by my father and I was never told the reason."

"Such matters are often confidential – what did Janus say to you at that time?"

"That he was breaking our engagement...it was a few years after he left Fort Temper before I saw him again."

"And what happened in the meantime?"

"My father passed away," said Valerie, looking down. "And I married Mr. Mayer."

"And Roman Janus? What became of him?"

"He took up the profession of...investigating supposed 'occult' disturbances."

The prosecutor beetled his brows and cleared his throat. "You sound rather dubious of such a profession, Madame – I take it you did not believe in such things?"

"Well, I was certainly *open* to a good many things concerning Roman," the woman responded, "but when we met again after so long and I told him of my father's passing, I felt certain that he... that he..."

"Yes, Madame?"

"That he might allow me to *talk* with my father."

Sounds of derision arose from the audience. Spiritualism had had its day some years ago and to hear that one of the Elite still might find credence in such well-worn fads, well, it was hard for some to stomach.

"And was he able to, ahem, bring your father around for a chat?"

Valerie Havelock-Mayer's eyes narrowed and her mouth tightened. "No," she whispered. "No, he *refused*. And I knew then that this entire 'spirit-breaking' of his was nothing more than a charade."

From her table off to one side, Janus stood up once more and puffed out her chest.

"Valerie, you go too far this time!"

The judge silenced the entire courtroom again and warned my companion that if she spoke out of turn for a third time, she would be held in contempt of court. Why he believed that would stand as any sort of deterrent to someone already on trial for murder, I couldn't say. Alas, it seemed to quiet her and the prosecutor continued with his questioning of Valerie Havelock-Mayer.

"Madame," he said, pointing, "do you know the defendant in this case?"

The woman shook her head, gazing at Janus. "I admit I do not, save that I know that she has taken up residence in Roman's house and has been using his car...and, good Lord, his clothing!"

The counselor gripped the lapels of his coat and swiveled around to look at Janus himself. "When you were interviewed some days ago by the Mount Airy Police Department, you stated that though you did not actually know the woman personally, you had your suspicions as to her true identity. Is that not so?"

"Yes," admitted Valerie, shaking her head.

"And who do you believe her to be?"

"Objection!" bellowed my companion from her table.

"Overruled!" the judge yelped. "Answer the question, Madame Havelock-Mayer!"

Valerie's piercing glare was enough to ignite the very air, I thought.

"A lover of Roman Janus' – from before we were engaged to be married."

While the crowd around Wendy and me thrummed with murmurs and whispers, the prosecutor thanked the woman and asked her to step down from the stand. When Janus waved her right to cross-examination, he then called his next witness.

Wendy excused herself, but I barely noticed; I had been rattled and rolled by the parade of information.

After a small army of witnesses brought on to testify that Sgt. Janus had not been seen in almost a year – a café owner, a book dealer, a suit-maker, and the like – the man next called a Mount Airy police officer to the stand.

I had a feeling that the tempest had only just begun.

"Please state your name for the record, officer."

"Deputy James A. McPeek, badge number four, Mount Airy Police Department."

The officer seemed a solid sort, sitting erect on the stand in his crisp, clean uniform and holding his helmet in his lap. I sensed that he was a no-nonsense type, the kind you could trust for facts.

"Deputy McPeek," said the prosecutor, "were you personally acquainted with Sgt. Roman Janus?"

"Yes, sir. I first met him more than a year ago, but had been aware of his investigations long before that. I helped him on one such occasion last April."

"Good man, was he?"

"He seemed to me to be so, begging your pardon for the opinion."

"No, no," the man admonished McPeek, "I asked for an opinion and you gave it. Now, have you ever known Janus to disappear for this long of a stretch?"

"No, sir. Not that we keep tabs on him, but he is an acquaintance of my captain, and I've never known my captain to have remarked before about the sergeant's absence."

"As well as being one of the arresting officers, you were also part of the team of investigators who searched Janus House this past week, were you not?"

McPeek nodded; I caught a hint of reddening in his cheeks. "I was."

"Please tell the court what you found there, Deputy."

"Well, we didn't find the sergeant, if that's what you mean."

Titters came from the audience. The prosecutor scowled. "Quite. But I believe you know what I mean, officer."

The deputy shifted a bit in his seat and ran a finger along his pristine coat collar.

"We found blood, sir."

I could scarcely believe my ears. I looked around for Wendy, but she was only then coming back into the room, walking over to our seats.

"And where did you find this blood, Deputy McPeek?"

"In one of the automobiles at the house. A Lincoln."

"And have you seen this vehicle before, sir?"

McPeek glanced around at the judge, the jury, and at Janus herself.

"Yes. I have seen Sgt. Janus driving it, as well as that woman there." His pointing finger indicated my companion. She looked as if the deputy had just thrown a snake at her.

I was trying to sort it all out in my head. The blood had to have been mine, or even Janus'...I mean, of course, the female Janus. Good God, was I confused! But overriding that confusion came a sense of great wrong-doing, for I knew that the police were operating on a false assumption, one that would paint an innocent person as a murderer.

"Young man, what do you mean by this?"

I arrived back in reality to find the judge gesturing at me with his gavel, and every set of eyes in the courtroom upon me. Wendy was tugging at my coat sleeve.

I had stood up in outrage without being conscious of such an action.

Sitting back down, I mumbled an apology and waved my hat feebly for the trial to continue.

The prosecutor thanked Officer McPeek for his testimony, Janus once again passed on cross-examination, and the judge called for a recess in a state of high irritation.

Out in the lobby, I asked Wendy what she thought of it all.

"It's a damn farce," she replied without hesitation. "Valerie's taken center stage, a spot she's more than familiar with. She'll railroad your friend right into the noose."

"Do you actually believe any of what the woman said?" I inquired, chewing my lip. My leg ached like the dickens.

Laying a hand on my arm, Wendy's face took on an even more serious cast. "Joshua, I've known her long enough to tell you that *she* believes it. Every bit of it. This is very, very personal to her."

"Another woman," I mused, feeling as if two trains were headed toward each other on the same track and I was in the middle of an oncoming revelation. It hurt my head a bit to stitch it all together so I began to hum a jazz tune I liked to derail it for the moment.

Above the proceedings, though, and beyond, I couldn't shake the sensation of being watched.

A smartly-dressed man accompanied by two uniformed officers marched up to me and asked for a minute of my time. I realized with a start that it was the same man who arrested my companion a few days previous, Captain Mumford.

"Like to ask you a few questions," he croaked, looking me up and down. "Mister...?"

"Hargreaves," I told him, irritated by his presence, "Joshua Hargreaves of Canal Chichester, if you must know."

"'Fraid I must, sir. It's very important. Can we step outside?"

Wendy, bless her soul, intervened by introducing herself and asking if it was so very necessary at that moment. Mumford blanched a bit, then frowned.

"Well, Miss Jackson, I suppose we could wait until, ah, after the trial's done for the day," he said. "Please don't be so hasty to leave, Mr. Hargreaves, eh?"

The man turned on his heel and he and his two lackeys disappeared into the crowd. Wendy smiled and took my arm and we re-entered the courtroom.

The feeling of being watched only intensified.

As we sat waiting for the judge to take his bench once more, several items danced before my eyes. The forbidden room, the file on Sgt. Janus at Fort Temper, the God-Stone, the disk that drove men mad and broke spirits…it was more than a mere mortal like myself could credit, let alone work like puzzle pieces to fit into a larger, complete image.

Simply thinking on them all provided a contest between my head and my leg as to which could ache the more.

I watched a bailiff approach the judge and speak to him. I focused on his moving lips and strained my ears – something about "Miss Smith" not able to be found?

Alarmed, I began to rise to my feet. Then, the defendant herself drifted into the room escorted by a court officer, looking paler and more drawn than I'd ever seen her before.

Janus looked as if she was dying by degrees.

I attempted to catch her eye, to silently impart some solidarity to her, but more so as to try to relate my unease over the ever-growing and disconcerting feeling of being watched. My companion did not look up, just stared off into space, presumably awaiting the continuation of her trial.

When the prosecutor stood up again, he led another procession of witness to the take the stand and relate what they knew of the woman who was accused of murdering Sgt. Janus. There was one of the actors used in the filming of *A Woman in the City* at La Maison D'Havelock, Lord Harry Christmas of Christmas Hall himself and his wife, and others, all of them called to give testimony on the strange female who announced herself as Janus and acted as if she were *Sgt.* Janus. Little was said about spirits and hauntings; I thought it wise of the prosecution to avoid that tangled knot.

More witnesses followed as the afternoon wore on, most of them tradesmen of one kind of another who reported that calls to Janus

House had ceased almost a year before and that they had been afforded no explanation as to why their services were no longer apparently needed.

Janus watched it all through slitted eyes, barely moving or showing any signs of interest. I wanted to scream at her to say something but she sat there and allowed it to transpire. It was painful to view.

"The state calls Holden Francis Muir to the stand."

The name tickled at my memories; why did it sound familiar?

A man was escorted in by four uniformed policemen; he was shackled like a prisoner, both by his wrists and at his ankles. Once a handsome chap, he'd obviously fallen on hard times.

Then it hit me: Muir. I watched a man named Muir die several days before, a lieutenant at Fort Temper and a member of the Order of the Blood Red Rose. The prisoner being trotted out into the courtroom bore a resemblance to the lieutenant and I then remembered that Lieutenant Muir had said he had a brother...

When Holden Muir was asked to raise his hand and swear on the Holy Bible to tell the truth, he snorted, sneered, and did it anyway, though in a kind of half-hearted manner. I could tell he'd once been a dandy, but now carried a peculiar malevolence that pervaded the courtroom.

"You served with Sgt. Roman Janus, both at Fort Temper and in the field?" he was asked, after the preamble of establishing the man's identity. "Knew him well?"

"Indeed," came Muir's simple reply. "For many years, through thick and thin."

"You also know the former Valerie Havelock?"

The prisoner nodded. "Yes. Bit of a chip off her father's old block. We all hated him you know, and ol' Val was his daughter more times than not."

"Did Janus speak of his relationship with Major-General Havelock's daughter?"

The judge sighed and leaned forward on his chair. "Is this going somewhere, Prosecutor?"

The attorney blinked several times. "Yes, Your Honor. We hope to establish the defendant's identity and illustrate a motive behind her crime."

My companion did not object, at least not verbally; I saw a light come into her eyes and her ears perk up at the exchange.

"No, to answer your question," Muir announced, getting things back on track. "Roman wasn't a talkative chap, not when it came to his personal business. We, his brother soldiers and I, didn't hold much with his supposed romance with ol' Val...we knew he carried the torch for another."

Valerie Havelock-Mayer rose from her chair like a specter, ready to begin shrieking and waving her arms. Someone next to her pulled her back down and she sat there, fuming.

The prosecutor paced back and forth in front of Muir, wringing his hands. "Now, I assume you have some proof of Sgt. Janus' interest in this other woman? He spoke of her? Showed you her picture?"

Muir was quite obviously on the verge of laughing at that. "Oh, Heaven forefend, no! I mean, yes, he spoke of a girl back home or somewhere, had that certain gleam in his eye when he did, but he didn't care much for photos. Roman was a superstitious sort...no, not true, actually. He didn't like photography, said it 'took something from you,' but it was more than just superstition. He *believed* that."

"Did Major-General Havelock interfere with the soldiers' personal business at all?" asked the prosecutor.

"Oh, quite often," Muir grinned. "Nasty man. A tyrant's tyrant. A *controller*, if you know what I mean. Loved the riding crop. Didn't like Roman from the first, but that changed when he became engaged to ol' Val. The man acted like he'd adopted a new son – but that all changed, too."

"*When* did it change?"

Muir's face took on a satanic light. "When Roman broke the engagement. And then our dear commander threw him out of the service, lock, stock and over-the-barrel."

"You know," sneered Muir, "they're going to hang me any day now. Little matter of a murder."

"Yes," said the prosecutor, nodding. "You were found guilty in the death of one Darwin Fetters. You murdered him at Janus House more than a year ago. There have been some delays with your execution, but I understand it to be finally and firmly scheduled."

"Good boy," Muir replied. "So, I have nothing to lose by breaking a few rules and spilling some military secrets. Now, Roman Janus *loved* stories – would you like to hear a story?"

The judge sat back and rubbed at his temples. Then, after a moment, he lifted his chin to the prosecutor and silently gave his approval. I sat on the edge of my seat, so entranced was I by Holden Muir and his charisma. Wendy's hand snaked into mine, but I barely felt it.

Janus sat still as a statue, her eyes locked on something invisible.

"We were in the trenches," began Muir, "caught in some crossfire and left twiddling our thumbs while our tanks cleared out a nest of the enemy's that was giving us so much trouble. Some of the lads were giving Roman some good-natured guff about ol' Val, but he just kept smiling and touching a spot on his tunic over his heart. I knew then that he had another sweetheart and his hand-holding with Havelock's spawn was just play-acting. I know the look of a man in love and my friend had that look and more when he placed his hand over his heart.

"So, when the shooting stopped, we pulled ourselves out of that hole and made for the enemy's last position. We were getting a bit stale out there; hadn't had a decent *kill* in days before that. Funny thing about ol' Roman, though…no one ever saw him kill any of the enemy. Regardless, he was right with us, rifle in hand and helmet on straight and leading the charge. He was a sight. Got us right up to our target and told us to fan out and clear the entire scene.

"It was a small copse of trees we'd come upon – not sure what they were but they were runty things, all short and scraggly. No leaves; it was almost winter. Anyway, Roman has me stick with him and we trot into the thick of those trees and start looking around. We had each other's backs. Nothing to worry so overly much about. Then, I hear the sergeant gasp.

"Now, Roman Janus was a man who didn't gasp much. Little on this Earth could faze him, except love, obviously, but on that day I heard him lose that damned composure of his when he saw something ahead of us. I peered through the mist that hung around the trees like cotton stuck to thorny branches and saw the soldier there."

Muir paused, his eyes scanning the entire courtroom. I'm not ashamed to admit that I hated him at that moment for his grandstanding.

"He was pinned to a tree," he continued. "Crucified with bayonets. Strung up like our Lord and oozing life. The enemy had left him there to die, probably run off by our advance. The bastards must have been in the middle of torturing the man. There was a slight rise and fall to his chest. He was still breathing…barely.

"Janus rushed up to him. Threw down his rifle and ran right up to the tree and then stood there studying the man as if he didn't know what to do. I came up behind him and tried to push him out of the way. I was annoyed by what I thought was his frozen inability to see if there was anything that could be done, but Roman Janus was a rock. I couldn't budge him. He threw up an arm to fend me off and it was like the branch of an oak. Almost knocked me to the ground, damn him.

"I watched as he cupped the soldiers face in his hands and leaned in to him. Took me a moment to realize he might have been listening to the soldier speak, but then it dawned on me that I was wrong. He was listening, but not for a voice. Then, Janus let go of the man's face, turned around, picked up his rifle, and then marched away. Already flummoxed, I saw in an instant that the soldier was dead.

"Later, back at our camp, Janus was beside himself. Never saw the chap so livid. Said to me that he couldn't 'reconcile such cruelty delivered upon one human being by another.' I said to him, 'That's just war, my boy,' and tried to shrug it off, but our sergeant was changed that day. Changed forever.

"Then, he disappeared."

The soft sounds of sobbing came to me as I digested the story.

Who was weeping I could not say, because I didn't bother to look. I was transfixed by the images Muir had conjured.

"Where had he gone?" asked the prosecutor. "Had he permission to—"

"No," stated Holden Muir firmly. "Away without leave, if you can believe it of ol' By-the-Book Janus. Just ran off, and for *weeks*. And in the *winter*. Then, one day, he materialized at the front gate of Fort Temper and marched his way up to Havelock's office. I found out later that he'd broken off his engagement to the Major-General's lovely daughter."

The prosecutor frowned, perhaps expecting an outburst from Valerie. "And your commander was displeased?"

A wicked grin spread over Muir's face. "Oh, he was downright beside himself. Dishonorably discharged Roman and swore the man's name would never be mentioned on the premises forever more, plus a day for good measure…"

"For his desertion of his duty or for his daughter?"

Muir looked up to the ceiling. "Good question. Why, for both, I presume. Our dear commander was a bastard for all seasons – his anger was all-pervasive and encompassing."

"Were you able to glean anything at all from Roman Janus when he returned to the base? Where he'd been? Who he saw?"

"He said very little to *me*," Muir sneered. "I was only his *friend*, you see. Mentioned something about 'skating near Potshead' or some such. He was like a ghost when he came back, like all the life'd been drained away from him. Like he wasn't all there. Met up with him again a few years later and we renewed what I laughingly call our friendship – Roman was a bit more solid then. He'd taken up with all the mumbo-jumbo 'spirit-breaking' romantic trash and—"

"Quite," said the prosecutor. "Mister Muir, have you ever seen the accused before?"

His long arm snaked out and he pointed to my companion. The prisoner raised both eyebrows and turned to her, as if confused as to why exactly he was in the courtroom.

Rarely have I ever seen someone so struck by the sight of another.

Holden Muir gasped and covered his mouth with one hand. Leaning toward Janus, he studied her with eyes as wide as saucers.

"B-but..." he sputtered, shaking his head from side to side. It was strange that he had not seen her when he entered the room, but after only a few minutes with the man will tell you that *everything* is about him.

Janus rose from her seat, staring at Muir. Her face was cold and composed, in direct opposition to the livid fear that had seized his features.

Then, he started to laugh.

And laugh. And laugh. In an instant, Holden Muir was hopelessly insane.

Once the prisoner had been seized by the bailiffs and hauled out of the room – his laughter still echoed in my ears – Valerie Havelock-Mayer was asked to take the stand once again.

Wendy's hand tightened in mine and I looked over at her, quietly assuring her I was still sane myself. The worst was still to come, you see.

The prosecutor asked that Valerie confirm Holden Muir's story of the events at Fort Temper. This she did, though it was plain that she did not relish it, seeing as how she had lost the man she believed she would marry and settle down with for the rest of her life. And for what? Another woman? Someone who Roman Janus had known and loved *before* herself?

"And the, ahem, crucified soldier, Madame? You can confirm that, also?"

Valerie only shook her head, and vehemently so. "I...I have never heard that story before today," she whispered. "Roman did not explain himself after he came back...from his desertion. But I *knew* what had happened. A woman knows these things."

The prosecutor stepped closer to her; he'd reached the core of the matter, or so he believed. I could see it written across his smug face, a face I wanted to dearly bruise at that moment.

"And what was it that you knew? Or know now?"

Valerie Havelock-Mayer stood up and turned to face Janus, a towering figure in crimson, like something out of the Old Testament.

"*She* is the reason that Roman left..." Valerie pointed one, long lacquered fingernail at my companion. "And *she* is the jealous and jilted lover who *murdered* him!"

Madame Havelock-Mayer was not through with her pronouncements. Oh, no; she was not. Before I knew what was happening, the woman swiveled around as if on a phonograph turntable and cast her pointing digit at yours truly.

"And that man there is her accomplice!"

The prosecutor, as smug as the day is long, offered an oily smile to the courtroom.

"I call Mister Joshua Baines Hargreaves to the stand."

Well-done, I thought. I complimented them silently; the prosecution team had done a thorough and professional job of it, and they'd played it as a trump card. It all made sense, in a twisted way: Janus, a woman with no memory of her past life, accused of the murder of a man who was most likely more a nuisance to the community than a boon. And myself? Her willing partner in crime, quite possibly awed by the murderer's beauty and charm and bamboozled into her scheme of revenge on her former paramour.

It all sounded like a dime novel. Yet, still, I was a character in it. If I was to take the stand, they would accuse me and convict me and I would never, ever get to the truth of the dark lady who arrived in my little hometown so many months before and changed my life forever. I was prepared to fight to get to the bottom of it, if that was what was necessary.

Wendy seethed at my side, and began to rise up in indignation, no doubt a tart rebuttal on her pretty lips. I pulled her back down, but she released my hand in anger and clutched instead at her skirts.

I stood up and addressed the court.

"Your Honor," I bowed, "and you fine members of the prosecution – I respectfully decline the invitation. I do not wish to testify at this time."

The judge nearly spit nails. "You can't do that! Bailiff, seize that man and bring him down here!"

Yes, it was to be a fight.

The audience erupted. I couldn't have asked for anything better at the moment.

Cries of both outrage against me for my cheek and support for my civil disobedience rang throughout the room as chairs scuffled across the floorboards and fists pounded against walls and banisters. Someone grabbed my shoulders from behind and I saw uniformed men yelling to have me held fast as they made their way toward me.

I planted my cane on the top of the head of whoever had grabbed me. Receiving a satisfying grunt of pain, I found myself released. Then, the room swirled into a downward spiral of chaos.

Looking for Wendy, I also found that she was gone.

Don't ask me how, but I somehow made my way across the room and to the door, feeling for certain that if I had hesitated a single moment I wouldn't have left the area sans shackles. A few men – and perhaps one woman – went home that night with sore midsections and bruised jaws, but it couldn't be helped. I was fighting not only for my own freedom but that of my companion's, too.

Down the hallway I flew, or as swiftly as my aching leg allowed, and then I was out the doors of the courthouse and stumbling down its steps.

A raucous honking assaulted my ears and I looked up through a cloud of dust to the most-welcome sight of Miss Wendy Jackson driving up to me in a sporty flivver.

"I appreciate you taking the time to actually brake and stop," I told her as I climbed into the vehicle. "Jumping onto moving automobiles is a game for those with two good legs."

"Where to, Cap'n?" she shouted over the din of the engine.

Looking up at the courthouse and imagining the face of Janus and her intoxicating eyes, I settled myself in the seat and prayed she'd understand my actions.

"To Potshead – and step on it."

While on the long road to Potshead, Wendy offered a sobering thought.

"Joshua," she said above the wind, "perhaps by uncovering her identity, she will no longer be the person we've come to know."

I had no real answer to that, so in the grand tradition of my incarcerated companion, I remained mute. As it turned out, Wendy's words were more or less prophetic.

Thankfully, the village we sought was tiny; Wendy knew the area somewhat and we were glad to discover that exploring it shouldn't take much time, seeing as how small it was.

Potshead seemed to have no real purpose, or if it ever had one that was lost in the mists of time. Its scarce inhabitants just *were*. They were neither farmers nor laborers, just a collection of homes and faces and complacent presences.

"It doesn't exactly scream at you, does it?" noted Wendy sagely. I congratulated her on her aplomb and we alighted from her motorcar. Looking around, I contemplated knocking on doors and simply asking if anyone knew a young woman fitting Janus' description. If only I had a photograph of her at hand...

A man walked toward us from the nearest house. He was dressed plainly and appeared to be in the neighborhood of seventy years old. I sensed neither welcome nor annoyance from him. Wendy asked me if I wanted her to speak to the man, but I stepped forward and made to greet him.

"May I be of aid, travelers?" he said, with the slight accent of the outer territories. His eyes flicked back and forth between Wendy and me.

I informed him, as best I could, of why we'd come to his village and described Janus to him – the female version, that is. The man's face changed, suddenly very sad.

"Aye." The man nodded and set his mouth in a tight slash. "Aye, I knew of her."

Finally and at last.

The man invited into his home and we accepted with a vision before us of great mysteries to be solved and justice to be wrought.

I shouldn't write this down, as it is mostly personal and not germane to the chronicle of the adventures of "Lady Janus," but I'm compelled to do so anyway.

Once we bade our host goodbye and returned to Wendy's flivver, she sat there behind the wheel and gazed at me in a queer fashion. Uncomfortable under such scrutiny and drained from the knowledge that had been imparted to us, I asked her why she looked upon me with such mixed emotions.

"I feel like I'm in a jazz tune," she whispered. "All up and down and back and forth."

"I said the same sort of thing to *her*, not long ago," I informed Wendy. "You like jazz, do you?"

She leaned over to me, all sweet-smelling and rosy-cheeked. "I like *you*," she told me with a saucy smile.

The rest I shall leave to your imaginations. I am a gentleman, after all.

Back in Mount Airy, I allowed myself to be taken into custody.

The trial had been suspended, I discovered, while the authorities had searched for us. Now, with me firmly in hand – they let Wendy go after she raised a ruckus – the farce could continue.

With thinly-veiled malevolence, the prosecutor informed me that if I were to testify under oath, that my "transgressions" might be excused. To wit, I would not be held in contempt of court and I would be doing the community a good turn. Meek and humble, I agreed and looked forward to my time on the stand. There was much I had to say.

Wendy and I had been gone for two days, and the judge was fit to be tied, so the trial resumed on the third day and I was called to the stand – in handcuffs – and asked to place my hand on the Holy Bible, etc., etc. Once we got through that, I was seated and the circus began.

"Do you know the accused, Mr. Hargreaves?"

"I do, but only for a few months."

"Do you know Sgt. Roman Janus?"

159

"Only by reputation, and not overly so at that."

"Have you accompanied the accused on several, err, journeys over the past few months?"

"Yes. I am her chronicler, you see."

"Quite," spat the prosecutor. Then he skewered me with a pointed look, apparently about to offer a quick thrust that would have me on the spit and ready for the fire.

"Do you deny that she and you conspired to *murder* Sgt. Janus and usurp his home and property?"

"Of course I deny it," I returned, smiling. "It's patently absurd."

"And why do you say that, Mr. Hargreaves?"

"Because," I told him with somber certainty, "the dead cannot murder the living."

This perplexed the man, as I'd hoped it would. The audience gave out with a collective expression of bewilderment.

"I caution you, sir," the judge growled, "to not make light of these proceedings. If you cannot explain your comment, I shall lock you into a cell for a long, long time."

My moment had come. I found Wendy's pretty eyes in the crowd and then Janus' own orbs, strikingly different, but compelling all the same.

"The explanation is simple, Your Honor, Mr. Prosecutor – the accused cannot have murdered anyone. She has been deceased for some years now."

I was not through. Turning again to look at my companion, a wave of sadness came over me; I had entered the courtroom with a triumphant air, but then, on the verge of the winning circle, I remembered what my new-found knowledge actually meant.

"Isn't that right…Nocturne?"

The name caused a stir in her, as if she was a basin of water and I had dipped my hand into it and swirled it about.

"The love of Roman Janus' life," I continued, "resided in Potshead. Her name was Nocturne Planchette and she died in a sledding accident. Janus deserted his post at Fort Temper to return to her after he'd witnessed the horrific event on the battlefield, as Holden Muir told us. I have spoken to her father and he swore to me that it is the truth.

"Roman Janus was never in love with Valerie Havelock. Perhaps we'll never know why he entered into an engagement with her, but he broke that agreement after the death of Nocturne – during that very same illicit visit."

I paused, looking over at Madame Havelock-Mayer. Tears streamed down from her eyes and her mouth moved, not from actual speech but from inarticulate rage. Like father, like daughter.

"I offer to this court my own supposition: that Major-General Willis Havelock did knowingly and willfully bring about the death of Nocturne Planchette."

The prosecutor, snatching futilely at his full wits, gasped out a single word.

"Wh-why?"

"Because," I told him, "I suspect his ire over Janus' desertion of his duty and his daughter was more than he could bear. And he knew where the sergeant was heading. A man like Havelock does not allow his daughter to consort with a mystery. The major-general would have found out everything he could know about Roman Janus."

A voice spoke up from behind me.

"Thank you, Joshua. Satisfactory. Most satisfactory."

Everyone looked to see the accused standing there, apparently composed once more, but I could see her hand tremble and her bottom lip quiver ever so slightly. She was shaken, and I regretted everything I had to say out loud in that courtroom.

She approached the judge. The man actually reared back a bit, like a hiker from a snake.

"If the prosecutor is finished, may I call my first witness?"

The judge looked over at the state's attorney, dumbfounded. The prosecutor simply walked backwards until he bumped into his table and then sat down behind it without a word.

I vacated the stand and placed myself at my companion's table. The show wasn't ended, not quite yet.

Janus approached the witness stand and, after pausing to stare at it for a moment, then turned to the audience.

"I call as a witness," she intoned in a clear, loud voice, "Major-General Willis Frank Havelock."

I think it's fair to say that everyone present looked over to the empty seat and half-expected for the man in question to appear there; after all, stranger things had already happened in that room.

Janus spoke again, perhaps even louder, her voice ringing out like a bell.

"Major-General Willis Frank Havelock, you are being called to take the stand as a witness! You are called to give testimony! Appear!"

A chill ran up my spine. What was she doing? The request was purely meant for show, wasn't it? She couldn't *call up* the dead, only put them to rest – or was I wrong on that score?

"Order! Order!" yelled the judge, finding his place in the book that had been opened in his courtroom. "You will come to ord—"

His gavel was knocked from his hand and flung across the room to thump against a wall. An angry red welt appeared on the man's hand and he clutched at it in obvious pain.

My attention was then drawn to my companion. A dark patch of something flew toward her from the judge's bench and past her face. She flinched and I saw a crimson slash across her cheek, bloody and dripping.

Havelock. Riding crop.

Good God, *no*.

Shrieks arose from the gallery. Men shouted. The prosecutor was knocked over like a bowling pin, savagely and swiftly. The stenographer's head whipped back as if she'd been struck soundly in the face.

"Wendy!" I yelled, "Get out of here!"

Though my wrists were bound by manacles, I sprung over to Janus and tried to push her to the floor. Instead, she cut my legs out from under me, sending me sprawling. A strong wind blasted over my head and I swore I heard the sound of deep-voiced laughter.

"Havelock," screamed Janus. "Face me!"

The disk. She didn't have the disk. She had slipped it to me when

162

she was arrested and it was back at Janus House.

I feared for her then. Whatever the force was in that courtroom, it was highly disturbed. It meant to do her great harm – and possibly the rest of us, too.

Objects sailed through the air, creating a miniature cyclone; at first smaller things, then furniture. The deafening sounds of chairs and tables being forcibly slammed into walls and smashed against the floor were horrendous. I could barely look up into the maelstrom.

Janus screamed. I tried, oh Lord, I tried to help her, but I could not move. My lady kept her feet, that much I could still see, but she was being battered around like a child's doll. And she kept screaming.

Then, another voice, piercing the chaos.

"Father, *no!*"

And then it all stopped.

I crawled across the floor over the debris and destruction. Havelock's spirit – if indeed that is what it was – had been broken by his own daughter. But it wasn't Valerie I was concerned with at that moment, but the woman she had accused.

When I found Janus – no, *Nocturne* – she was still standing, incredibly enough. But when I finally saw her face, any sense of relief vanished.

Numerous cuts and scrapes were tattooed across the skin of her cheeks, her jaw, and her forehead. Her hair, which had begun to grow back, was missing in places.

Her eyes were dull and glassy, no more the multi-faceted metal whirligigs I had known.

Her mouth hung open. She did not speak. I hugged her to me, sobbing her name. Then, she collapsed into my arms, insensate.

Despite my leg, I picked her up and looked for a path out of the room. Moans of shock and pain assaulted me, but I ignored them as I stepped over and in between piles of rubble that defied description as the normal artifacts of human life. Nocturne did not stir as I jostled her along.

Once again I made my way to the corridor and to the courthouse's doors, not knowing how I managed such a feat. We seemed invisible to the incoming knot of people who entered the building to rescue and recover what they could.

I stood outside and stopped, unsure of nothing else but my desire to help my friend. She seemed suddenly very light in my arms, as if she weren't there at all. I looked to make sure I wasn't dreaming.

"Here, put her down on the seat, Joshua. That's a good boy. Yes, there…"

I don't remember Wendy pulling up to the curb in her automobile. I don't remember actually placing Nocturne in the back seat of it. I don't recall in the slightest taking my own seat and Wendy taking hers.

I do remember the sight of the girl, though. Wendy was a mess, but somehow she still looked pretty. Thank the Lord she wasn't hurt.

"To Janus House," I directed her. "Quickly."

There was no cheekiness then from Wendy, no witty repartee. She put the flivver in gear and pulled away from the curb. Then, from out of nowhere we saw a flash of red. A figure stood in the street, blocking our way.

Valerie Havelock-Mayer.

Walking over to my side of the automobile, the woman glanced at me and then at the prone, but still open-eyed figure slumped in the back seat.

"I want to go with you," she said, and placed a hand on my arm. There was no steel behind it, but a desperation that took my breath away. "My beliefs…have been shaken."

"Get in," I told her.

As we drove away, the four of us, completely unbidden, a particular jazz tune sprang to mind. The discordant bits were all coming together. And I had to make something more of it.

I had to save Nocturne. I had to bring her back. And with utter certainty I knew how. A shadow on the wall had once pointed the way.

I had to enter the *room*.

Chapter VIII

THE ROOM

Dear Sir,

I present to you the final adventure of Janus, as chronicled by Joshua Hargreaves, First and Only Chronicler to the Spirit-Breaker.

This account follows the seven chronicles I have previously sent you and which, I trust, you have already read. I take full responsibility for their veracity, of course - if there is any question on any point found within the accounts, I ask that you please take them up with me personally.

I am not the man I once was.

No one with any claim to humanity could experience what I have and not be changed by it. I am not asking for pity or sympathy, but rather simple understanding for any gaffes or missteps I may have taken throughout the course of my time alongside the woman who called herself Janus.

I shall endeavor to restrain from waxing poetic in this account and get right down to the particulars of the events that unfolded once I returned to Janus House after the trial of my companion.

We – myself, Wendy Jackson, Valerie Havelock-Mayer, and the unconscious Janus – drove into the midst of a camp of our enemies on the grounds of the house. I thought it damn peculiar when I spotted the group of people once I turned off the road and onto the driveway, but then realized who exactly they were: Followers of Havelock from Fort Temper.

They rose up *en masse* when they spied the car, more than twenty of them, and made it clear they meant to block our way. I saw the glint of gunmetal among their ranks and the way they stood shoulder to shoulder and knew that no good would come of my slowing down to ask them what they were doing there. They sought revenge, naturally, for Janus' entombment of the God-Stone and for the death of their fellows.

Angry, I pressed the gas pedal to the floorboard and raced toward them. Valerie gave a startled cry and Wendy gripped my arm as the Lincoln churned toward the men of the Order of the Blood Red Rose.

Perhaps they saw the daughter of their late leader in the motorcar or maybe they thought it unwise to make a racket, but they did not fire upon us. Not caring to repay such a kindness, I stayed the course and drove right into the lot of them, yelling for the ladies to keep their heads down.

Angry curses and yells of protest rang through the air as some of the cult members leapt from the path of the Lincoln, but there were a few thuds of impact. I did not care; the men were fully responsible for their actions as I was with mine.

Nearing the front steps of the house I did not reduce my speed, but slammed on the breaks and spun the wheel. The automobile skidded sideways across the grass of the lawn and I thought we'd flip over for certain. Luckily, we remained upright and once the Lincoln had come to a full stop, Valerie and Wendy jumped overboard and made their way up the steps.

I scooped Janus up into my arms and followed after them. Shots rang out and wood splintered around us – apparently the ban on firearms had been lifted.

I nearly flung my companion through the air to the ladies as I scrambled to be free from carrying her and able to pull my pistol from my pocket. From the doorway I fired several times without aiming, in the hopes that by returning fire I'd give them pause and allow me to move inside and secure the door.

After I did just that, I wedged the door shut with a large wooden coat rack and then used a sideboard from a nearby sitting room to barricade the foyer door.

We'd barely a moment to catch our breath when the windows all around us exploded into a million pieces.

"Farther in!" I ordered the ladies and we moved ourselves to another room. I knew from experience that all other ways of ingress would be locked and that the house could serve as a fortress when needed – at least for a short while.

We convened a war council at the base of the grand staircase. Checking on Janus one more time – we'd laid her down on a comfortable-looking settee – I turned to Wendy and Valerie to gauge their own states-of-mind.

"We do what we need to do, Joshua," said Wendy, squeezing my hand in a gesture of solidarity. "Can't say much for your choice of friends, though..."

Valerie would not meet my eyes with her own. It was strange to be so close to her, to be on the same side with her, so to speak. She was very beautiful, in a cold fashion, but I could see that something had been altered within her, something she once valued and could no longer rely upon.

I asked her if she were truly with us, telling her in no uncertain terms that we needed to count on her, that it wasn't a fight of our choosing but one that demanded our full attention. Valerie had made a decision to come with us, yes, but I had to know that, come what may, she was to be trusted.

"Yes, Mr. Hargreaves," she said after a long moment. "I recognize some of those men out there – the ones trying to kill us – and I know what they are capable of. My father...kept only the very best around him and I understand that they won't hesitate to finish what they've begun."

Then she looked over at Janus. An odd expression molded her features into a surreal portrait of the woman; it was almost frightening to see something other than haughtiness and derision there.

"This...woman," said Valerie. "What can be done for her?"

Came a loud crash from the vicinity of the front rooms. I jumped over to the door and flung it open to peer into the area.

A bottle with a rag stuffed inside it and the rag burning.

The bottle had come down in a small stone fireplace. Frozen between making the leap to snatch it up and throw it back outside and slamming the door shut on its deadly potential, I hesitated far too long. The bottle exploded.

I came to a minute later, spread out on the floor in front of the stairs and with Wendy kneeling next to me and slapping my face. Sitting up, I tried to surge to my feet but dizziness knocked me back down.

"We can't stay here," Valerie insisted. "The next room's afire. Thank goodness it's mostly stonework in there, but we cannot stay *here* and wait for it to spread."

"Upstairs," I croaked and finally found my feet again. "I think the house can fend for itself, but if not, we'll be safer upstairs."

Picking up Janus once more – she barely weighed anything – we mounted the stairs and began to climb them to the second floor. Passing a window that looked out fully upon the side yard and partially on the front lawn, I witnessed a sight that should normally have fortified me but then only chilled me.

The local constabulary had arrived.

The dark vehicles of the authorities pulled up one by one, and the lead one disgorged Captain Mumford. The men of the Order took a few steps back from their siege of the house and regrouped, most likely to present a unified front.

The police captain strode over to the bunch and one of them broke away to meet him on the little cobblestone path that leads to the front steps. When they came within three feet of each other they both stopped and began to converse.

The Order man gestured toward the house and each time he did, Mumford looked in that direction, scowling. I didn't care for it at all; we were wanted by both parties and if the soldiers, or whatever they were, from Fort Temper spoke well and laid it on with a honeyed tongue, we'd soon have double the trouble than before.

"I can go out and speak to them," Valerie said in my ear. "*All* of them."

I weighed that option. Madame Havelock-Mayer's standing, her position in the community – I began to think it could work in our favor.

She must have certainly guessed that I was pondering the possibilities. "At the very least, I may gain you some time," she offered.

I looked to Wendy for her agreement. The girl nodded at me, solemnly.

"Go," I said, "but be careful."

The woman apparently thought that was an odd notion coming from me, but I fixed a smile on my face to assure her. "I wish you no ill, Valerie. You've…seen what I've seen. There's another world out there."

She patted my hand, sketched a quick hug with Wendy, and she was off.

"Now what?" the girl inquired.

"Now you lock yourself in one of the upstairs bedrooms and stay out of sight," I told her, hefting Janus in my arms and starting back up the stairs again. "I have to take her somewhere."

It's to Wendy Jackson's extreme credit that she did not argue with me on that score, only kissed my cheek lightly, then Janus', and fled up the stairs and 'round a corner. Within seconds I heard a door slam and the bolt being thrown.

I took another direction, heading toward the forbidden room.

Determined not to become lost on the way to the room, I checked myself at every turn and made certain I was going the right way.

Janus did not stir the entire time and I felt the oppressive weight of the situation upon me. She was fading away before my eyes, becoming more insubstantial with every passing second. I wanted to cry out, to beg for her life, but the words would not come; I had no idea to who I would ask for such a boon.

Finally, I entered the corridor of the forbidden room and ran to its door.

Janus I deposited on a long couch that stood against the opposite wall. In the dim light she seemed only an outline of a person, pale and almost transparent. I waited a moment and her form appeared to solidify. Looking back at the door over my shoulder, I knew that there was no time to fritter away with pointless worry. I had to *act*.

With a last glance at her face, I embraced an impulse and pressed my lips ever so lightly to hers. They were cold and dry and lifeless.

"Please forgive the impropriety of my kiss, my lady," I whispered to her still, unmoving features. Then, I stood and stepped over to the door.

The knob felt slick against my palm, as if polished and waxed, yet it looked old and in need of attention. Twisting it, I found that the door would not open.

This rocked my back on my heels. My heart pounded in my chest and my temples throbbed; was I to be stymied in the one thing I wanted most in the world at that moment? Who or what was conspiring against me in my attempt to save the life of...

But *no*. Not life. Nocturne Planchette was dead, wasn't she? I was too late – and by several years.

An idea came to me suddenly, one borne from the depths of my desperation, perhaps. I lifted up my companion once more and brought her to the door. Then, I took hold of one wrist and placed her hand over the door knob. Still holding her, I pressed her fingers around the knob and twisted all as a single unit.

The knob turned and I heard the bolt recede. The door was finally open to me.

I lingered on the threshold, clutching Janus to me. The doorframe held nothing but black within it. Cold, dark *nothingness*. To step into it...it simply didn't seem possible.

Closing my eyes, I stepped forward, angling my companion so that we would pass through the doorway together with one motion. I expected some sort of change to occur, I guess, a sign that we had moved *through* something, but no such sensation came to me. A solid floor met my foot as I stepped into the room; otherwise nothing was altered in my immediate surroundings.

Save, of course, that I was within the room that I had been forbidden to enter.

The sound of the door closing behind me came to my ears, yet it sounded as if in another part of the house. This did not startle me, amazingly. If I was to never again exit the room in order to save the woman I cradled in my arms, so be it. I was prepared, or so I believed.

I hesitated to open my eyes, despite the growing heat of completing the mission I'd laid out before me. When I did open them, I doubted my own senses: the blackness around me was absolute. You may laugh, but I tested the function of my eyelids by closing them and opening them in rapid succession. Except for the normal sensation of movement from such an act, there was no difference.

I felt as if I knew at that moment what it was to be blind.

Panic crept up upon me, vying for my attention. I was resolute in my commitment to not give in to it, for I had much to accomplish and would not be deterred from my path – though that path had become increasingly obscured. Pushing back against the fear, I arrived upon a moment of clarity. Still I could not see, but the rest of my senses became heightened. I could hear a kind of hum in the room, a low, steady tremor that spoke of a great machine of sorts. Then, with my tongue, I could taste the air about me, cold yet not icy, and with my nose I captured the exceedingly slight tang of some exotic incense, the variety of which escaped me.

Suddenly, I could feel again, my sense of touch returning all at once. There was no sensation of the cloth of my companion's clothes on my fingertips and palms.

Janus was gone.

Panic assailed me once more, urgent in its insistence. I flailed about with my arms, angry that I did not feel her weight gone from me at the moment – I presume – she was taken from me. But why did I feel as if she were *taken* from me? I reconsidered and came to the conclusion that the woman was simply *no more*. There was no other rational explanation for it.

I was lost. Despair replaced panic and with it came an irrational sense of failure: I had lost my companion in a room that had been bared to me and within which I could not see. If the door still existed behind me, I could not credit it. The room had swallowed me whole; I expected to be consumed at any moment like Janus.

The darkness persisted, unabated. My eyes did adjust to it as I hoped they would. Perhaps that was a foolish hope, but I had clung to it with little else to cling to. The hum was still present, as was the strange tang in the air and the coldness that did not chill me. I grew irritated after several minutes – if time actually passed in that room – and I set my teeth into that irritation. It seemed wholly me and I cherished it against the pervasive weight of the darkness.

Finally, and fully ill from the waiting, I called out into the impenetrable black.

"Hello? Is there anybody there?"

The walls of the room abruptly faded away. I say this, though again you may find it odd, for up until that moment the reality of their presence flittered about on the edge of my perception. If not for the still-solid floor beneath my feet, I would have guessed that I'd been suddenly hurled into the void of space through the act of speaking aloud.

Then, a sound. Faint, but I could discern it above the alien hum. At first I was not certain that I wasn't imagining it, but as it grew somewhat fuller in tone, I was sure of its existence.

Footsteps. And coming closer.

I called out again. Where the boldness of my voice came from, I do not know. Receiving no reply, I listened to the footfalls again; they were definitely drawing nearer to my position with a clear, mature sound to them – it was no child's gait. An adult approached and, I assumed, male.

"Hello?" I did not shout it that third time, but spoke in a normal tone of voice. I expected an echo for some reason, but there was none.

The footsteps ceased. I felt a presence. Not in front of me or behind me or even to one side, but *all around me*.

"Are you there?" I asked. "I heard you approach. Who are you?"

Damn it, but I was sick of being blind! I'd managed to keep my speech free from nervous vibrations, but being sightless and engulfed by strangeness had taken their toll on me.

I heard then the sound of breathing; not labored or sickly, but the clean passage of air through a set of nostrils and the occasional deeper inhalation and exhalation of breath. Someone was…considering me.

"Why do you not speak?" I inquired. "Surely you must know that this is all very strange to me…won't you at least tell me who you are?"

Silence. Then, a voice. Fluid and manly it was, pleasing to the ear yet of a commanding nature, too.

"I am Roman Janus," it said. "It is a pleasure to meet you."

The floor was still there, though I felt as if it had been swept out from under me.

"What are you doing here?" I asked when I had found my voice again. I burned with questions, though the immediate desire to save Janus – no, *Nocturne* – also burned within me, too.

"Sleeping, resting," said Roman Janus slowly. "Contemplating."

Silence again. Then:

"Nocturne, you say?"

I felt as if I'd set a lead ingot before someone, then suddenly turned it to gold before their very eyes.

"Yes, dammit," I hissed, growing irritated again. "What *is* this place? Is it life…or death?"

"More of the anteroom between the two," he said, sleepily. I tried to summon up an image of the man in my mind, to go with the voice, but my inner eye failed me.

"I had her with me just now," I told him, "when I entered this room. She had forbade me from entering, but—"

"You say she was *with you?*"

"Yes," I insisted, "with me, but she is *dying* somehow. We have had a series of…of adventures and—"

"Impossible," pronounced Janus. The word lay there with leaden finality.

My anger increased. "You have no business saying what is and what isn't impossible! You have not lived with the woman for the months I have!"

"There is no living!" he boomed. "Nocturne is dead!"

173

I collected myself after that, holding my tongue and afraid that his voice would recede and not return. I gathered my thoughts and my feelings together and made another go of it.

"She appeared in my village, Canal Chichester, several months ago," I began, with a tone that I hoped sounded conciliatory. "She had no memory. But she was drawn to...spirits. I helped her lay several to rest, or so I believe. At any rate, *she* believed it."

"Canal Chichester," he said. "I was born there..."

"Yes, I know. So was I."

"Your name, sir?"

"Oh, goodness; how rude of me. Hargreaves. Joshua Hargreaves."

I pictured a smile coming to his face; that mental image was very strong.

"My mother was a Hargreaves," he explained. "How I miss that place....adventures, you say?"

I felt as if perhaps his mind was being focused, bit by bit, by conversing with me, but I could not afford to become too optimistic about the situation. I was on queer ground.

"Sgt. Janus," I said, "there is a crisis, outside in the...the house. And beyond. And Nocturne...is there nothing that can be done? She came here often, to this room, and afterwards it was like she was refreshed somehow, as if she were being healed..."

"No," announced Janus. "I cannot help. I cannot leave this room. I am sorry."

I was undeterred by what I was hearing. I would not stand for it. Despite the darkness, I balled my fists and swung them at the air in a silent fit of rage.

When that subsided, I spoke again.

"Can't you at the very least save Nocturne?"

When the sergeant's voice issued forth again, it came from a single source; that is, the man was almost standing in front of me, or so it seemed.

"As I have said, Nocturne is no more," he whispered. "She died years ago. Because of my foolishness. I vowed that she would always be with me thereafter, in my heart, but corporeally she is gone. I mourned her for a long, long time…"

"She was very much like you, or what I imagined you to be like," I told him. "She…became you. Some even…saw you within her. How could that be possible?"

Janus thought on that. I heard his footfalls again, as if he were pacing the floor in the room.

"Good Lord," he said abruptly. "Good Lord, could it be?"

I asked him what was the matter. A hand gripped my shoulder, causing me to jump.

"Anima and animus…Joshua, is it? Don't you see, lad?"

"'Fraid I can't see anything," I told him. "But isn't that the—"

"Yes!" he enthused. "Yes, man and woman, woman and man. Good Lord, how stupid I've been. All those years…oh, my good, sweet Lord…"

He began to weep.

Never before had I felt such an outpouring of deep anguish, of bottomless regret. The man was experiencing a grief that cannot be quantified; so strongly did it manifest that my own eyes welled up with tears and I felt then through empathy as if my entire world was crushing down upon me.

And there was nothing I could do. At that very moment, I realized with shocking exposure that Nocturne was gone forever.

When his chasm of grief had been crossed, Janus returned to stand before me in the total blackness of the room.

"Joshua, I sense that you are a good man," he said. "I would like to show you something. Come with me, please."

His hand once again took my shoulder and we began to walk. My first steps were hesitant, for I did not feel certain that the floor continued beyond the place where I stood, but Janus guided me in a fashion and after several steps we stopped. Then, I heard the sound of a doorknob turning and hinges creaking.

A breeze touched my face. Again, there was nothing to see save darkness, but I knew that another room or space had been opened up before me. And the feeling there was an expansive one.

"Let me show you what I've been contemplating," said the sergeant.

Together, we walked through the doorway. Beyond that I saw... forgive me, but I must meditate a moment on the words to set down in the next passage.

Beyond I saw stars.

Thousands of pinpoints of light broke through the inky black to make themselves known. The spread across my vision like a spangled blanket and stretched to the very limits of my perception, in every direction possible. It was not as if I was looking at a wall of them, but rather I was looking *through* them; there was an enormous sense of *depth* and *length*. It nearly took my breath away just to look at it, and it was all that I could do to clutch to my physical being and not have it whisked away as if dust before the imponderable movement of the universe.

I asked Janus what I was looking at.

"Life and death," he said. When I did not reply, he continued, his voice sifting through the darkness.

"You see there, Joshua? How the stars on the wall do not so much twinkle, but appear and disappear?"

I told him that yes; I saw it, now that he directed me so. But a wall? It was more a living thing, I said.

"A wall, nonetheless," he told me. "You may perceive it slightly different than I do. Regardless, the stars that appear—"

"Are life," I offered. "And those that disappear?"

"Death. The cycle of life and death lay there before us. Each star representing a living being's path. This is what I have been studying."

The utter immensity of it was staggering. It could only be a dream, or so I reasoned with myself. What else could it be?

"Where...where am I?"

"Ah," he said, somewhat bemused, "that is something we cannot know. How we can even see *this*," I imagined him gesturing to the wall, "is beyond my divination. I have found that we should not question it, only view it and try to understand it."

He paused for a full minute.

"Now do you know why I cannot leave the room?"

I tore my all-too mortal eyes from the wall. "You must," I implored Janus. "You're needed. Out there."

"No," he sighed, "I'm not ready. Not healed."

I flailed about, trying to grab hold of him, but if he truly had a solid form I could not find it.

"Coward!" I screamed. "Nocturne set wheels in motion – *you* set them in motion, and you have to finish the job!"

"You try my patience, sir," he rumbled in a dark tone. "I am recuperating, as I've told you. The world outside dealt me a mortal blow and I have no desire to return to it in haste."

His words seared me, so ridiculous did they seem. "Malarkey! I even saw you pointing the way to the room one night – the house itself led me to it on more than one occasion! And now you say you will not return?"

Suddenly, my hands connected with something. A body. An arm, a shoulder.

I aimed a punch beyond the shoulder and my knuckles connected with bone and flesh. I heard a surprised grunt of pain. *Good*, I thought – let him hurt like I hurt.

Silence.

The stars dimmed around us. I thought I saw half-lit shapes swirling around in the darkness.

"Well done, Mr. Hargreaves," said Janus, finally. "Well done, sir. My Lord, what a blow."

"There's more where that came from," I told him, though uncertain of the veracity of it. "Now, will you come back with me, Roman Janus?"

He did not answer at first, but I sensed that he stepped past me and toward the wall of stars. Then, what seemed to be a hand passed in front of one dim star and around it.

Came a whisper. A name.

"Nocturne..."

The hand came away from the bit of light and left behind only deep,

177

cold black. The mood in the room shifted, feeding me with electricity.

"Right," said Janus. "Let's go. We're needed."

Once more gripping my shoulder, he led me away from the wall, through the doorway and across the floor to the outer door.

"I may be a bit rusty," he noted, and opened the door. A bright rectangle of light appeared before my eyes: the corridor of Janus House. Silhouetted in that doorway was the figure of a man, my companion, Sgt. Janus.

"We'll be lucky if they haven't burnt down most of the house by now," I told him, ready to step through. "Let me bring you up to the present as we move along—"

"*No*," said an unfamiliar voice in my ear.

What happened next is, unfortunately, almost a complete mystery to me.

I remember hearing the voice and rocking back on my heels at the sound of it. Janus grabbed my arm, but if the gesture was to steady me or steady himself, I do not know. After that, well, I wasn't myself, or so the sergeant has told me.

My mouth opened of my own accord and my jaw made a small cracking or popping sound, as it often does. That, too, I remember. Then there was a powerful rushing sound that filled the air around me and tore my very breath from me. I could not breathe and my head began to swim. The bright rectangle of the doorway began to spin, and I believe I was lifted up off the floor. At the very least, I could no longer feel it below me.

I heard another voice then. It took me a moment to realize it was my own, yet somehow amplified and with a dual quality. In fact, it was as if someone else's speech overlaid my own, speaking the same words.

"Janus," it said, "you're not going anywhere. Close the door."

I became aware of what I would call a presence, another entity besides myself and the sergeant. Almost as soon as I came to that conclusion, I came over all hot inside, as if a fire had been lit in my belly and the flames whipped up all of a sudden.

I was lost once again. I'd been robbed of my body.

Janus' voice came to me from far away. It shouted a name: Havelock.

The heat of the major-general's presence burned at me, but I was too far away to care. There was a moment when Janus tried to pull me back from…a precipice? A cliff? But I resisted, only wanting to steer clear of the conflagration. Let the world burn; I had seen the stars and only wanted to join them.

I remember the sense of a struggle occurring and of the give and take of a fight. My name sounded again and again, and each time it jolted me from my impending slumber.

Rallied, I attempted to pull *myself* from the brink.

Havelock's voice came to me again, but from all over, not just in my ear.

"Lay down, boy," it commanded, and I shrank from it, instinctively. "You're not fit for it. You're a weakling. You're not a soldier."

This struck me in an odd way; wasn't I? Hadn't I trudged along in lock step with Lady Janus? Hadn't I been in the middle of several battles? Hadn't I received *wounds*?

I spat at the man. Something hissed all around me. "You had Nocturne killed," I told Havelock. "*You* couldn't stand for her hold on Janus…"

The presence raged at me. Somewhere else, another presence cried out in its own anger. A truth had been let loose upon the ears of a victim of a horrendous crime.

"*Damn you, lay down!*"

I wouldn't. I didn't. I decided to fight, as a soldier would.

My memory truly falters here, at that moment. I saw flames, actually *saw* the fire, but stepped into it. After that…I only remember what seemed to occur a million years after that.

A white hot light punched through a veil that hung over my eyes. A circle of illumination, intense and startling.

A disk. I looked at its face.

Havelock screeched. Claws raked at me, shredding me. The blood leaked away from my body.

"Joshua! Hold on, lad! Hold on!"

Then, stillness. Someone leaned over me. A dark figure, a silhouette. Reality rushed back in and revived me.

"Was that..?" I asked.

"Yes," Roman Janus nodded.

"From where?"

"My pocket. How astounding."

I sat up. We were still at the room's threshold, just inside it. I could not see Janus' features, but he seemed solid enough.

"Havelock?"

"Gone."

"Because of the…disk?"

"Yes."

"Let me look at it."

He held the artifact up before me, its surface plain to see. The light of it had softened a bit, but it still glowed with its own inner illumination.

There, in its depths, I saw an *eye*.

"Is that…?"

"Yes," said Roman Janus. "The Face of God."

I wanted to blink, wanted to feel blasphemous for daring to gaze at it, but I couldn't, even if I tried.

"How?" I asked, my mouth dry.

"The room," he replied. "Somehow, it allows it here. Now I know what it is, the disk. And it makes perfect sense to me, though I'm only mortal."

"Tell me," I implored him.

Janus sat back. "The Face we cannot look upon in life, outside this room, for it brings only madness in its Divinity. To the dead, it is a reminder of their inescapable path, and the ties that bind their spirit to the earth are torn asunder when they are forced to look upon it."

He paused. "It all makes sense now," he whispered. "All of it. The disk, Nocturne, Havelock, my very nature…"

"The house," I said, remembering the rest of it. "Wendy…err, a girl. You don't know her. Or maybe you do? And Valerie! Valerie Havelock-Mayer!"

The man jumped up. "Valerie? Good God, here? Where?"

I pointed to the corridor. "Right out there, Sergeant. Where you're needed."

"I said it before, Joshua Hargreaves – let's go."

Then the face of Roman Janus appeared to me, as the light in the corridor grew to encompass both of us. There, I took in his countenance – roughly handsome, dusky blonde hair, eyes of verdigris – and it was good.

This was a man I could follow.

Disk secured once again in his pocket, the sergeant jogged off down the corridor. I joined him upon the stairs and we made our way toward the troubles below.

I had not, let me assure you, forgotten Nocturne, though.

He moved like lightning down the stairs and through the house – *his* house. It seemed to welcome him.

Before we reached the foyer from which wafted the sickly smell of burnt wood and fabric, Janus stopped and held out an arm to impede my own progress.

"Policemen and followers of Havelock?" he asked me.

"Yes," I nodded, "The Order of the Blood Red Rose. Most likely a bit piqued at the whole burying of the God-Stone incident."

"Hmm," he hummed, "you'll have to tell me more about that, of course, but later. For now, it should be me who confronts them. I'm betting my sudden appearance might actually clear up a few of the problems, eh?"

I could only agree with the man. Thinking suddenly of Wendy, I told Janus that I needed to gather her up and make sure she was well. He gave me a curt nod and walked over to the large set of double doors, beyond which we could hear voices in conversation.

I bounded back up the stairs, but paused at the first landing. Below, the sergeant threw open the doors – a bit too dramatically, I thought – and stepped through them.

Even at a distance, I could hear the sharp intakes of breath and the voice of Valerie Mayer-Havelock singing out Janus' name in blood-curdling disbelief.

After a few tries, I found the bedroom that Wendy had locked herself in and when she realized it was me, she flung herself through the opened door and into my embrace.

"He's returned," I told her, struggling to breathe.

"Who?" she asked, confused.

"Janus, my dear," I informed her. "Sgt. Roman Janus, Spirit-Breaker."

Stunned into silence, but handling the news better than ol' Val I should add, she took my arm and walked me toward the stairs.

"Might want to wait a bit," I said, holding her at the top step. "He's got a lot to clear up down there. And I have quite a lot to tell you."

Later, after all the players had been dispersed, I approached Janus as he stood among the ruins of his foyer and sitting room. Surveying the damage, the man shook his head and frowned.

"I suppose I deserve this," he said quietly, dropping a charred piece of wood onto the smoke-blackened stones of a fireplace. "Something to add to the price I'll pay for all of it."

I asked him what had been done about the men from the Order.

"The officers ran them off," Janus told me. "That's a loose end that I'll have to tie up at some juncture. But I can't worry about them now."

Emboldened, I inquired as to his involvement with the group. He only grunted and shook his head. I didn't press the issue. I had bigger fish to fry.

"Please, tell me, sir – where is Nocturne?"

Janus looked up at me with a look that might have been frightening if I wasn't bound and determined to wrest and answer from him. We stood there for several moments, staring at each other.

"Here," he said, tapping his breast. "She's right here, Joshua Hargreaves."

"That's not good enough, dammit."

"I've been told many times by many people," Janus said, seemingly ignoring my statement, "that if they would ever see a ghost, actually *see* one, their lives would be forever and irrecoverably altered. Has your life been altered, sir?"

His question took me by surprise, I'll admit. I didn't appreciate him changing the subject like that, but maybe he was the sort to play a game first, make a person jump through a hoop before answering the real question before him.

What could I say, though? I'd glimpsed a…mechanism heretofore unknown to mankind, an improbable concept that supposedly encompassed not only all life, but the entirety of death, too. What could I say? How could anyone respond to that?

Instead, I asked him a question.

"Do you like jazz, Sgt. Janus?"

He digested that for a moment, then gave me a slight smile.

"I think I understand, sir," he told me. "Indeed."

Not satisfied myself, I turned to leave. He called out to me.

"Joshua, turn and face me, please," he requested. I did so, not a little bit defiantly. He looked at me and narrowed his strange eyes as he did so.

"Ah," he whispered after a moment. "I think I understand something else now, too."

"What would that be, sir?" I asked him.

He took my hand and shook it.

"That we are both in love with the same woman. And that neither of us will ever forget her."

Janus stepped out onto the porch of his house to see us off. That was good of him, I suppose, but save for Wendy, I would have preferred to be by myself.

My charming companion offered to drive and I graciously accepted the offer; my leg was beginning to bother me again. I threw what little belongings I had at the house into the boot of the car and bundled myself into the passenger seat.

The last words of Sgt. Janus rolled around in my thoughts.

"What will you do now, Joshua?"

I suppose I'd have to think of something eventually.

With a promise that I would send the man the entire Chronicles of Lady Janus once I had finished with them, I walked away from

Janus House, most likely for good. Looking up at the porch, I saw Valerie come out the door and stand beside the sergeant.

She waved to us and then slipped her hand into his. He did not refuse it.

Wendy backed up the car and turned it toward the road. Pausing, she looked over at me, her saucy lips curling into a moue.

"What now?" she asked, apparently seeing something cross my face.

A thought had struck me, of something worth investigating. I turned to look at Wendy, one question on my mind.

"Do you believe in ghosts?"

'Ghost' Trapped by Janus, Police Say

A strange, vaporous mist appeared in a tenement on the 4900 block of Walpole Blvd. yesterday at approximately midnight, residents report. The mist allegedly formed into the semblance of a man and went striding up and down the corridors.

Mount Airy law officers were summoned to the site when one of the residents, Mrs. Hugh Hamilton, called them in to stop the "ghost" from making a "racket" and not allowing her and her three children to sleep. Upon arrival the officers found that while they could confirm a moving, transparent figure in the building from which the very loud sound of booted footfalls could be heard, they could not make the apparition acknowledge them or stop its actions.

Mrs. Hamilton then grew so frustrated with the officers over their lack of progress that she took it upon herself to call a friend who is an acquaintance of Sgt. Roman Janus of 4 Raynham Road. Janus is the so-called "specter-sniffer" who first made a stir with police several years ago. Although absent from Mount Airy public life for more than a year, Janus arrived within an hour and set about addressing the situation to the satisfaction of not only Mrs. Hamilton but the other tenement residents, too. What exactly the man did on the scene is not fully known by this reporter.

The police did not return any calls for more information about the incident. Sgt. Janus also did not return similar calls.

From *The Mount Airy Eagle*
Early Edition – Tuesday, February 28

Return of the Spirit-Breaker

At the very end of *Sgt. Janus, Spirit-Breaker* I relayed my sincere hope that readers might become attached to the character of Janus and that he would make his timely return. I'm very happy to say that with the reviews on the first book and the volume you now hold in your hands – or on your device – both hopes have been fulfilled. Roman Janus seems to have been embraced by his fans and so has returned to once again rid the world of specters, spooks and spirits.

Now, I'm going to let you in on a little secret: it's always been a two-part story.

Warning: If you haven't yet read both *Sgt. Janus, Spirit-Breaker* and *Sgt. Janus Returns*, I recommend you accomplish those tasks first before reading the rest of this. Here Be Spoilers!

So, my goal all along was to introduce you to Janus' world, get you acclimated to it, and then pull the rug out from under you by "killing" him off. I thought it'd be really intriguing to come in not at the beginning of a new hero's career, but rather at the end of it. In *Sgt. Janus, Spirit-Breaker*, the sergeant became weaker and weaker until he more than met his match in a horrific brawl with an ancient spirit…and disappeared. This allowed me to then forge him a new beginning. That was the plan from the get-go and, I have to tell you, it feels pretty darn good to have followed through on it and reach the sweet spot I'm standing in right now.

I also knew that I didn't want to bring Roman Janus back right in the opening pages of this second volume, but rather explore what it would take for our friend to reappear in the waking world. He'd lost his mortal existence after years of spirit-breaking and, frankly, he was terribly shagged out over it. Janus had to, basically, put himself back together piece by piece and, until such time as that occurred, there would have to be somebody to fill in for him until he was ready to return.

Enter Lady Janus.

One of the thrills I received from comments and reviews on *Sgt. Janus, Spirit-Breaker* was that many readers were curious about the mysterious "dark lady" that acted as Janus House's *major domo*. That was entirely satisfying for me because her story was one I wanted to tell in this book, *Sgt. Janus Returns*, and explain her role in Janus' life. Far from being just a wisp of memory or a shade meant only to lurk in the background, I wanted her to take center stage and, in effect, "be" Janus for just about the entire sequel. And so she has, and I hope you enjoyed her adventures.

Is Lady Janus/Nocturne gone forever? Well, Roman Janus himself has said that she lives on in his heart – whether or not she will ever materialize again isn't clear, but stranger things have happened. In fact, a *lot* of stranger things have happened in Sgt. Janus' world.

That brings us to Joshua. I must admit that I really grew to like and admire the kid. He surprised me at just about every turn as I wrote the book and his part in the proceedings just kept expanding and expanding, taking on a life of his own.

Joshua, to my amazement, is very much like me; that wasn't intentional. Oh, I know that a lot of writers say stuff like that and are probably just kidding themselves, but Joshua was originally meant to simply be Lady Janus' chronicler and nothing much beyond that. Then he started demanding more and more to do from me and became, to my mind, almost an equal co-star alongside our heroine. In *Sgt. Janus, Spirit-Breaker* I resisted the urge to bring in a "Dr. Watson" type of sidekick, but I hope you'll agree that young Mr. Hargreaves here was far more than that. I wonder what will become of him now that his job's been, well, eliminated? What would *you* like to see Joshua do next?

One of the things that worried me most while writing *Sgt. Janus Returns* was the idea of breaking away from the storytelling form of the first book, a "hook" that seemed to be somewhat unique and for which I received many nice accolades. But…I didn't want to repeat myself. Sure, that may in the end amount to hubris on my part, but I was dead-set on maintaining the tone and atmosphere of the first book while adapting a different storytelling device, that of a single, first-person narrator. If you really, really liked the multiple-narrator scheme, never fear! Come back for the third Janus book and you'll be soundly rewarded, I promise.

So, the stories of *Sgt. Janus Returns.*

The inspiration for "Dig Deep the Well" came from my lovely wife, from something that happened to her family on a property they once owned. An old well had opened up in their backyard one day and was found to be filled with junk from a bygone era, meant to fill the old hole up and hide it away forever. I guess Mother Nature had other plans. For me, it opened up some creepy possibilities for a story and a good vehicle to test our heroine right out of the starting gate.

"That Man Right There" was originally an idea for a *Sgt.* Janus tale, but I knew that I couldn't sit on such a fun concept for very long. To me, the Janus stories were in a bit of danger of seeming too old-fashioned, so I introduced some of that new-fangled motion picture technology and Lady Janus and Joshua were off to the races. The inspiration for this one was a real-life filmmaker who claims that while making his movie, he captured demons and ghosts and the like on celluloid. Google it; it's all true!

One of the regrets I carried with me from the first book was that we didn't get to spend more time in Janus House. I tried to correct that with "Cutting the Strings," a story that utilizes the Room of Visitation, a part of the house that I first brought to life in the serialized online Sgt. Janus story "The Lost Wife of Thomas Tan." The other point of the tale was to insert a little tension into the growing relationship between Lady Janus and Joshua – though I'm sure they didn't appreciate it very much as it was happening.

If you ever run into me at a convention or a show, ask me to tell you the secret of "The Whispering Wallpaper of Christmas Hall"… unless of course you've figured it all out for yourself. Maybe you did at that; you're fairly clever, aren't you?

If asked which story in the first volume is my own personal favorite, I'll usually cite "When the Rain Comes." That's the one where I really tried to creep myself out while writing it, and encountered a week's worth of rain to mirror the endless deluge in the story itself. I wasn't going to try and write sequels to any of the tales in *Sgt. Janus, Spirit-Breaker,* but something called to me to revisit the St. Georges' farm and bedevil that poor couple all the more in "Marching to Perdition." Silly me, I left them in far worse a state this time than the last time…

From there we raced along to uncover the source of the regiment or revenants that trampled all over the farm, and it turned out to be the "*Deus Lapidem*." I'm not sure what it is exactly that makes Christian mythology such a good source for fantastic fiction – could be my Catholic upbringing – but I love all that stuff and was always fascinated by the story of Jesus' last footprint on Earth. By the way, I made all that up about it supposedly being the reason why there are ghosts all around us…or did I?

"Just Like Jazz" and "The Room" are so intricately linked that I plotted them out as one big story. That was a rough time for me, to write those final tales and bring the curtain down on two characters that I had come to admire and care for. Oh, I know what you're thinking right now: "You've got a funny way of showing it, mate!" Well, we always hurt the ones we love, yes? Joshua will recover, eventually, but Lady Janus? Not so much, I'm afraid.

But, *pssst!* Sgt. Janus has returned! That's got to count for something, right?

See you in Book Three, Janus Fans!

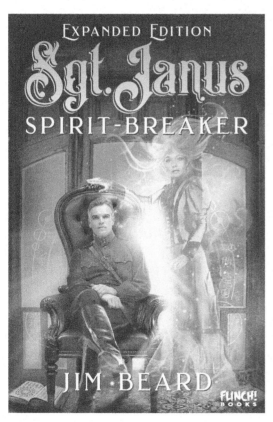

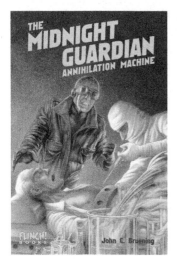

Made in the USA
Monee, IL
11 December 2021

84741867R10115